A TITLE TO MURDER:
THE CARHENGE MYSTERY

*Other Five Star Titles
by James C. Work:*

Ride South to Purgatory
The Tobermory Manuscript
Ride West to Dawn
Ride to Banshee Cañon
The Dead Ride Alone

A TITLE TO MURDER: THE CARHENGE MYSTERY

JAMES C. WORK

Five Star • Waterville, Maine

First Edition
First Printing: November 2004

Published in 2004 in conjunction with
Golden West Literary Agency.

Set in 11 pt. Plantin by Minnie B. Raven.

Printed in the United States on permanent paper.

Library of Congress Cataloging-in-Publication Data

Work, James C.
    A title to murder : the Carhenge mystery :
a western story / by James C. Work.—1st ed.
       p. cm.
    ISBN 1-59414-029-4 (hc : alk. paper)
    1. College teachers—Fiction.   2. English
teachers—Fiction.   3. Fugitives from justice—Fiction.
4. Heroines in literature—Fiction.   5. Missing
persons—Fiction.   6. Nebraska—Fiction.   I. Title.
PS3573.O6925T57 2004
    813′.54—dc22   2004050297

A TITLE TO MURDER:
THE CARHENGE MYSTERY

Chapter One

"Childe Roland to the Dark Tower Came."
—Robert Browning

It was one of those offices so modern and so sterile it made you feel like touching your hair to see that it was all smoothed down. I checked the knot on my tie and wished I had a sharper crease in my khakis. I closed the door, feeling a bit like a kid called into the principal's office. The lettering on the glass read:

WESTERN NEBRASKA COMMUNITY COLLEGE
Dr. Richard Venirs, Administrator

Or, if viewed from the newly carpeted and freshly painted hallway:

WESTERN NEBRASKA COMMUNITY COLLEGE
Dr. Richard Venirs, Administrator

The college offices lodged in one wing of Alliance's Library and Learning Center might lead one to expect a chilly and formal receptionist, but one would be quite wrong. The warm smile of the young lady behind the desk not only made me want to go back and comb my hair and press my khakis but pick up a dozen roses on the way. Take intellectual, poised, and perky and put them together and you have Ms. Jane Dorner, academic assistant to the administrator.

"Professor McIntyre." She smiled, looking up from her paperwork. The stress on the second syllable was a little joke we shared about my impatience with certain people who call professors Bob or Jim or Karen instead of Doctor Whistler or Professor Black.

I smiled back, and I'm not known as a man who smiles a lot. Not so much a dour personality as a face that more comfortably frowns, if you know what I mean.

"Miz Dorner," I joked back, seeing from the little oak nameplate that she hadn't changed her maiden name.

"You're early," she said. "We weren't expecting you until . . ."—she consulted a big appointment book that lay open on the desk—"two o'clock this afternoon!"

"I caught a tailwind crossing into Nebraska," I explained. "Made good time. I took a chance that Venirs might be free this morning so we could get the orientation interview over with. Maybe I'll take a nap this afternoon."

"Tailwind?" Miss Dorner said. "You flew to Alliance?"

"No. I towed the camping trailer. I'm going to live in it while I'm here. And when ol' Horse felt that westerly wind pushing us, he came sailing right along. I reserved a nice shady spot over at the Prairie View Trailer Park. It's close enough I can walk to campus."

"Didn't you like your accommodations last summer?"

"Oh, they were comfortable enough. But every time I came in the front door and started upstairs, Missus Samuels poked her head out of the drawing room to see what I was up to. I'm not real big on being monitored all the time. No, the trailer will give me some privacy. I can have a whiskey without worrying about a landlady getting a sniff of it."

"I hope it has an air conditioner. We're getting temperatures in the nineties."

"Air conditioner, microwave, cable TV. All the luxuries."

"And you're still driving the old Horse?"

Jane Dorner's contagiously playful smile encouraged my curmudgeon face into another grin. Last summer she "got" me where Horse was concerned. Got me pretty good, too!

Horse, my pickup, is a three-quarter-ton Dodge from the Triassic Period. I think his mother was a mountain wagon who met a 6x6 Army personnel carrier on furlough. Horse has rust and dents, and without a ton of gravel in the bed he bounces around like a turpentined jack rabbit, but he gets me places and usually gets me back. The seats are Naugahyde, slick and shiny. The steering wheel is too big and it's cracked in places. The shift lever is two feet long and sticks up out of the floor.

Last summer I had parked behind the Alliance Learning Center in order to load my stuff into the college van for a week-long field trip. Ms. Dorner had come out to inform me I couldn't leave my truck there or the police would have it towed away.

But it was summer session, I had argued. There were hardly any students or faculty who needed parking space. There were not only empty parking slots everywhere I had looked, but there was grass growing in the cracks of the asphalt.

"The bus is about to leave. I don't have time to do anything about it," I had told her. "I'll just have to work it out when I get back." I had handed her my keys. "Why don't you hang onto these in case the cops want it moved. Or, you could take him home with you. In fact, you could get him an oil change and check the transmission fluid while you're at it. He could stand a good vacuuming, too."

I had been joking, of course, trying to get her goat by pretending to be a macho chauvinist who believes that a woman's place is in the passenger seat. Ms. Dorner had stood there with the keys in her hand as I waved from the departing van. She had met my big grin with an arched eyebrow.

That evening she had lifted her bike into Horse's rusty bed, fired up his big V-8 engine, double-clutched his clanking transmission into gear and bounced him home with her. During the week she had taken Horse to the QuickyLube, treated him to fresh oil and transmission fluid, washed him down, vacuumed him out, and had him waiting at the Alliance Learning Center when I got off the bus.

However, Horse had paid for all this pampering. She had used him to haul three loads of tree trimmings to the dump and a ton of sand for her nephew's sandbox. Anyway, that's how I had learned not to kid around with Ms. Jane Dorner.

"How's my class shaping up?" I asked now. "Did we make the minimum enrollment?"

She took a file from the upright rack standing on the desk.

"This is the registration list," she said, deftly covering it with a yellow sheet containing handwritten names. "And this is the waiting list."

The move had been too quick. And even if it hadn't been, her face told me there was something amiss with that registration list under the yellow sheet. Sure enough, when I moved the handwritten list I saw the name.

Margaret Street.

"Not again!" I moaned. "Can't you convince her she's taking up space other people want? Look, give me your pencil. All we do is take this first name from the waiting list and put it where hers is, then take hers and put it at the bottom of the waiting list. Then you call her and tell her they made a mistake at the registrar's office."

"I call her? *You* call her."

A person like Margaret Street shows up sooner or later in every extension class, every summer class, every evening class, every class any college offers to the general public. Margaret buys the wrong edition of the book, but it doesn't matter because she never reads it. Margaret arrives late and asks what the class has done so far, or she arrives early and interrupts the professor preparing the lesson. Margaret argues with everything. She has a personal anecdote for everything. Margaret drops out of class halfway through the term when it is too late for anyone else to use the space. No explanation, no warning.

Jane Dorner gently but firmly pulled the pencil from my fingers and shook it at me. "Now, Professor," she said, "you know we can't just change class lists whenever we don't like someone."

"Worth a try," I grumbled.

"And she's not that bad. I think Missus Street really wants to take classes. It's just that she gets swamped with all the social responsibilities she has to face as the director's wife. She can't help it if she suddenly has to plan a huge dinner party or go with her husband to some week-long conference in Lincoln."

I saw a couple of other names I knew, but at that moment the eminent administrator opened the inner door from the holy office and manifested himself in the outer room.

"David!!" he said, as if my coming were a surprise. Months ago, when we arranged all this, he was on a micromanagement kick and informed me we would have a long "orientation interview" to spell out the college's policies and his own expectations and get me all sorted out before I began teaching. But that was months ago, and he had probably forgotten all about it.

"Dick," I said. "How have you been?"

"We were really pleased to get your letter saying you'd be willing to teach another course for us this summer.

Really pleased! The dean, the summer session director, everyone. Really pleased! And I understand you've worked up a new course as well! Let me tell you, more than a few of our non-traditional students were pleased to hear that. You're pretty popular with them, you know. They were hoping you'd have a new class so they could take it. Oh, they're just really . . . really. . . ."

"Pleased?" I ventured.

"Right!"

"I liked the sound of last summer's topic better," Ms. Dorner interjected. "I prefer reading novels. This summer it's all . . . what? Poetry?" She eyed the title on the registration form.

"Poetry," I said. "Romantic period. Coleridge, Wordsworth, Keats . . . those guys. Good stuff. You should have signed up last summer. Five novels in five weeks. It got pretty grim there toward the end."

"I did like the feminist overtones of it," she persisted. "In fact, I'm surprised you offered it. I'll bet you prefer poker and beer with the guys to an evening of Emily Dickinson."

"That would depend on which poems they were and who brewed the beer. As for wagering, Ms. Dorner, I wouldn't bet with you about anything."

Administrator Venirs's brow showed a furrow you could plant Nebraska corn in. Clearly he was trying to remember last summer's literature topic.

"Novels with women's names," I reminded him point-blank. "*Missus Dalloway. Madame Bovary. Ramona. Sister Carrie. Tess of the D'Urbervilles.* And for outside reading we had *Mary Barton, Moll Flanders, Clarissa, Pamela, My Ántonia, Lolita,* and *Jane Eyre.* I was going to add *Cinderella* and *Snow White* but there wasn't time."

"What did you call it," Ms. Dorner said, " 'Women Who

Are Novels', or something like that?"

"I called it 'She Is the Novel'. It was supposed to be a pun on H. Rider Haggard."

Venirs's forehead developed another corn furrow, so I explained. "H. Rider Haggard wrote a popular novel back in the Eighteen Eighties, called *She*. I thought it would be a pretty cute title, except that nobody got the joke."

At the time I thought of it, the class in novels named after heroines seemed like a good idea as well as a way to teach some of my own favorite books. But as it turned out, I had to fight for continuity every inch of the way. The novels came from different countries and different time periods, some written by men and some by women, some with one political point of view and some with another. But, except for the coincidence that all the books have titles that are women's names, they don't have much in common.

In the end, the summer class of mostly elementary and secondary teachers earning credits for their teaching certificates did find one thing the novels had in common. For lack of a better term, let's call it "protagonist bonding". I've experienced it before, a class in which many of the students go through a charismatic or magnetic identification with a fictional character, sometimes to the point where they can't talk about anything else and objective analytical discussion becomes very difficult.

Take *Moll Flanders*, for example. In lecture I wanted to stress the form and genre of the book because in 1722 it was a prototype; as one of the first English novels, it set important precedents. I also wanted to explain the 18th Century social background including the horrors of debtors' prison, prostitution in London, and the transportation of felons to the colonies.

The class, however, wanted to talk about Moll Flanders's "plight", her overwhelming greed, her fear of poverty, and her—heaven forbid!—marriage to her own brother. I remember one class session when they were totally fixated on the heroine's discovery that her son, sired by her brother, was alive and living in Virginia.

"The poor woman!" Sandra Allock had said in class. "To go through all that dread and anxiety about meeting him! Imagine what she went through! And then to find out what a nice, normal young man he had turned out to be."

"Maybe we could look at that scene using our cause-effect formula for determining climax and anticlimax in long fiction," I had suggested dryly, pretty sure I would be ignored.

"Professor McIntyre," Don MacArthur had interrupted, "do you really think a woman who has made a lifetime career of stealing . . . and who even married a highwayman . . . could really just up and repent and stop being a criminal? All at once, I mean?"

"Well," I had said, "she is almost seventy when she has that change of heart. I think the approach of old age has a certain effect. . . ."

Damn! There I had been, falling into the same trap, ignoring my lecture plan and gossiping about Moll Flanders like she was some kind of geriatric salvage job. Nuts!

That's how it had gone with each novel. When the five weeks finally had drawn to a close, the students and I agreed that we had read some "interesting" books and had some "interesting" discussions. A good percentage of them had got As and Bs, five or six had gone away with Cs, three officially had dropped the class—including Margaret Street—and one had disappeared. As for me, it was with a sense of relief that I had bundled up my ream of lecture notes and slinked back to my own university in Colorado.

* * * * *

The student who had disappeared was the one loose end about that summer class.

"What do you hear about the Deering case?" I asked. "Did she ever show up?"

Venirs and Ms. Dorner looked at each other. Why do people always do that, I wondered. Give any two people a question on a serious topic, and before they say anything, they look at each other like two kids being questioned by a cop.

"I saw Sergeant Houghton at the lumberyard the other day and he said he's still looking," Ms. Dorner said. "But it's been a year since the murder and they don't have a clue. There was a rumor about her showing up as a dancer in a club over in Kearney or Morris or somewhere. I didn't hear whether anyone looked into it."

"Nice guy, Houghton," I said. We had often run into each other last summer at his wife's café. And later he had called me at home to ask some questions about her, but I didn't know anything except that Cass Deering had been in the class and then suddenly stopped showing up. But we had had a long talk about it.

"In fact," I said, looking at my watch, "I just might go see if he's at the café or the police station and say hello to him."

"Don't forget these," Ms. Dorner said, crossing the room to bring me a stack of paper. "They're the hand-outs you asked for. If you want to leave them in the classroom downstairs, it's unlocked. And last week I checked with Adam's Book Shoppe, and they have copies of your text-book. Anything else you need right now?"

"That should do it," I said, taking the pile of hand-outs from her. "But Horse could use a wash and an oil change, if you have time."

Venirs looked puzzled a moment, then chalked it up to McIntyre peculiarity.

"You let us know what we can do," he said. "We'll just be pleased as heck to get you whatever you need. If the room isn't OK, or, you know, you need more hand-outs, you just say so."

"I'll do that," I said. I wasn't about to remind him about the orientation interview. When he turned to go back to his office, I winked in Ms. Dorner's direction and opened the door to the hallway. Summer session had begun.

The stairway was brightly lit and hospital clean. It led down into an equally antiseptic basement where the tiled floor echoed my footsteps. I opened one of the two heavy fire doors still shiny with factory finish and stepped into the commons area. Two pop machines and a candy dispenser stood at spotless attention against one wall. Drawn up to a half-dozen square Formica tables, four modern chairs were placed with military precision. Two stiff metal and fabric lounging settees faced the jet-black screen of a television set but looked as though no one had ever used them. The very air itself seemed untouched by human lips or lungs. In another day there would be students sitting in those chairs reading, students sitting around the tables drinking pop and scribbling at notebooks or engaged in conversations. The chairs would be out of place, the floor would be scuffed, there would be hand prints on the polished doors and stairway hand rails. But for now, it seemed impenetrably tidy and lonely as a dissection room at midnight.

I opened my classroom door and turned on the lights and a soft ambient glow spread over the two long tables and the lectern table at the head of them. The whiteboard—or whatever they call those new white blackboards—showed no sign of having been used, ever. The chrome and plastic student chairs sat expectantly on the carpet of light brown herringbone. It was clean, new, and scary.

Despite the fact that I've been teaching since schools were invented, that first moment in a new classroom still chills my spine. The straight rows of chairs before they get shoved into disorder, the spotless carpeting, the VCR and its monitor standing at the ready on one side of the lectern table, the overhead projector on the other, new marking pens in the whiteboard tray, the box-like lectern squarely centered on the desk—no matter how often I see it, and no matter how antique or how modern the room is, there's always a feeling about it that gives me stage fright.

It also gives me a feeling that I'm part of a long tradition. Sometimes I think I can sense the ghosts of dozens of generations of students sitting in those chairs and hear the phantom voices of a legion of long-gone teachers. But except for the low hum of the ventilation system, the room was silent and somber.

Back upstairs, I decided to go out the front doors so I could walk around the building to the parking lot where Horse was waiting. I wanted to see the front façade again. The building dominates a hill overlooking a park, and, whether it is the large turrets on the roof or the series of deep frontal arches, it looks like a modern brick rendition of a medieval fortified cathedral. Coming back to it, seeing the imposing entrance with its white turret, I recalled the ancient knight in Browning's poem, the surviving warrior returning to the crumbling ramparts in search of his ghostly colleagues.

What in the midst lay but the Tower itself?
The round squat turret, blind as the fool's heart,
Built of brown stone, without a counterpart
In the whole world.

I drove downtown, and, in spite of its being nearly noon, there were a half dozen empty parking slots in the middle of the business district. Horse slid into one of them as if he lived there. I left the truck's windows rolled down and my canvas briefcase on the seat, because I noticed during my stay last summer that most people in town seem to leave their cars unlocked. Maybe, if I were seen locking my truck, I'd be thought of as some kind of eccentric.

Ten steps down the street two plate glass windows flanked a recessed door. One window said **Houghton's Hut Café** and the other said **Breakfast   Lunch   Orders to Go.**

The moment I turned my nose toward Houghton's place I could smell hamburgers frying in their own grease. Opening the door, I smelled pools of rich ketchup next to fragrant hot French fries on heavy white plates and caught the aroma of industrial-strength coffee. There would be three kinds of pie in the pie case behind the counter: apple, peach, and blueberry. The blackboard over the pie case would announce **Today's Special**, which would be meat loaf on Monday, shrimp basket on Tuesday, spaghetti with meatballs on Wednesday, Mexican burritos on Thursday, and, in deference to Catholic senior citizens, tuna casserole on Friday. I can recommend the meat loaf and spaghetti, but the shrimp are fairly flavorless and the burritos are about as Mexican as corned beef. As for the tuna casserole, let's just say I'm glad I wasn't born a Catholic.

I had noticed a police car parked across the street, so I wasn't much surprised to find Bob Houghton, sergeant of police, having lunch in the booth next to the window. His wife Betty was sitting opposite him in the booth, tallying her cash register tapes with a hand-held calculator.

Houghton grinned at me and put down his ham sandwich to give me a handshake.

"Well, son-of-a-gun," he said. "Here's the professor again! How y' doin', Doc?"

"Sergeant. Missus Houghton. Nice to see you."

"Here," Betty said, sliding farther into the booth and dragging her ledger and register tapes out of my way, "let me make room for you. So, you're back to have another go at teaching teachers, huh?"

"I'm afraid so," I said, sliding into the booth next to her. "I just can't stay away from this nice warm climate."

Houghton gave me another grin and the waitress came to suggest I take the special. She also said I should have Pepsi instead of coffee, as the morning coffee was getting "sludgy".

"OK," I said. "Make it a Pepsi."

Betty asked about the class, and told me how sorry she was that she didn't have time to take it, then went on to describe her weekly schedule. Besides running the café, she kept a local 4-H group running, taught a Sunday school class, chauffeured the four Houghton kids to after-school activities, and volunteered at the local nursing home as a book reader.

"And I don't know why," she said, "but after supper I just feel too tired to go to a class. Funny, isn't it? But I bet your class is full, anyway."

"With a waiting list."

Sergeant Houghton began filling me in on town activities as if he felt I needed to be brought up to date. It made me feel good, as if by returning for a second summer I had somehow become part of the community. Not a total stranger, at any rate. He told me about the new police car, which he had assigned to another man rather than keeping it for himself. He mentioned that the local mechanic, Dale, had been hospitalized. Last summer, Dale and I had spent a few hours together under Horse's hood, trying to find out why the engine would stall in wet weather. And there was new paving down at the railroad crossing, and two new teachers at the high school, one in math and one in physical education, and Betty's waitress, Edna, was going out with the new math teacher.

There was a pause in the conversation. Betty nudged me to get out of the booth so she could go back to work. Bob asked her to bring him another handful of potato chips; in reply she leaned over and patted his tummy. No extra potato chips.

"I'm curious whether you found out anything more about Cass Deering," I said.

"Not much," he said. "One of her friends . . . her best friend, I guess . . . told me she had been pregnant, but lost the baby. But that was earlier. We're pretty sure she was living with that guy who was murdered. . . ."

"You still think she killed him?"

"Oh, yeah. Her prints were on the knife, and she left bloody prints on the wall and on the linoleum next to the body, even in the bathroom where she washed her hands. And there weren't any other prints anywhere, except for the victim's and the landlady's. I'll never forget seeing that body. Around here a cop sees dead guys every once in a while, but they're mostly from car wrecks. I've seen two that were shot, one by accident and one on purpose. And one who hanged himself in the basement. But that guy lying there on the floor in that apartment, dressed up like he was going out to dinner . . . big ol' carving knife sticking straight up out of him . . . never forget it."

"But still no sign of her?"

"Nope. We tried to use ol' Jafre's hunting dogs to track

her, but there was too much rain that week. And then wind and heat. I told you all that on the phone. Oh, wait a minute! After I phoned you, a couple of weeks later, some kids hunting jack rabbits found her charm bracelet in a field east of Highway Eighty-Seven, a little way north and east of Carhenge. A long ways from where she lived."

"You're sure it's hers?"

"One of the charms had 'Cass' engraved on it, and another one had 'CD' on it, so I'm pretty sure it belonged to her. Quite a few people had seen her wearing one like it. What beats me is how it got clear out there."

Part of my brain, I have to confess, was not listening to Sergeant Houghton. It was soaking in the olfactory delights of a genuine hamburger deluxe that had just been delivered hot from the grill to the adjoining table. It was the kind of hamburger where the cook puts the bottom half of the bun on the meat while it cooks so it will get all warm and greasy, then puts the top of the bun right on the grill where the hot steel will crisp the edges of the bread. That kind of hamburger comes with a quarter-inch thick slab of sweet white onion that had been growing in some local garden patch a day ago, and a slice of lipstick-red tomato dripping juice and smelling of warm summer days. For an extra twenty-five cents you get a square of Velveeta cheese melting over the meat patty under the tomato and onion. There isn't a fast-food burger in the world that can stand up to the real thing.

The other part of my brain was processing visual images of Cass Deering as she had looked in class last summer. I thought I remembered the charm bracelet, or at least the sound that such a piece of jewelry would make. She was a pretty young woman, buxom, smiling, and smart—and you got those impressions in exactly that order. The first thing you noticed was that she was small-town, unassuming, a kind of fresh-and-scented-soap pretty. Then you noticed nature had endowed her with a bosom that seemed too mature for her years—although exactly how old she was, I couldn't say. I'm rotten when it comes to estimating people's ages.

Her smile came easily and went everywhere and made you forget the bosom entirely; it was that good a smile. And when you listened to what she had to say, you realized that here was one smart young lady. She was not widely educated, but well read and schooled in the College of Experience, and had an uncanny ability to see into the core and meaning of most literature. She wasn't a schoolteacher like most of the rest of the summer class. Cass worked at outdoor jobs, sometimes on local farms, sometimes delivering orders for the auto parts store, often working at the little greenhouse attached to the lumberyard.

I should say that I suspected Cass Deering had more than an average intellect months before I even saw her. Our acquaintance began soon after Professor Henriette Palmer persuaded me to apply for a summer exchange program in which some Nebraska community college would send a teacher to do a course at our university and I would go do a course at theirs. Being a government program, the pay was pretty good. And the territory was new. So I applied, proposing the overly ambitious course in novels with women's names for titles.

Let's see. It was late October, I think, or early November when the college published its tentative list of summer offerings. Within two weeks Cass Deering wrote to me for the book list and syllabus. I didn't have a course outline written yet—I tend to put off doing it until the week before class—but I sent her a book list.

Then began a series of curious e-mails, about a week apart. She used the computer Internet connection at the town library to ask me all kinds of questions about the books, which she was reading quickly and with intense interest. Her questions were smart and fresh, not the stiff "what the teacher expects" kind of questions.

In Virginia Woolf's *Mrs. Dalloway*, Clarissa Dalloway has a passion for planning parties. It's about the only thing she is really good at. When an acquaintance named Septimus Smith commits suicide, she seems to envy him, and everything indicates that she finds her socially centered life unhappy and unfulfilling, even superficial.

Cass's letter about *Mrs. Dalloway* made me think she knew an actual person who was like that. I felt that the novel had caused her to see something in that person's life, something disturbing. That seemed the direction her intelligence took, moving from literature directly into life, and then into one particular life that the novel had shown her. Novels to her seemed magnifying lenses she held up to life, lights suddenly turned on to reveal the unrealized.

Even without knowing her, I worried she might be reading too much into the material. I'm often leery of extra-sensitive people who use fiction as a hiding place from life by projecting the characters into actual acquaintances, and then involving themselves personally in trying to solve their problems.

In class I found Cass Deering to be just as inquisitive and thoughtful as she had been in her e-mails. At times she seemed to drift off into deep contemplation of something some other student had said. But then, about halfway through the term, the man who shared Cass's apartment was found with a carving knife sticking out of his chest and Cass was nowhere to be found at all.

Chapter Two

Thou, whose exterior semblance doth belie
Thy soul's immensity
"Ode: Intimations of Immortality"
—William Wordsworth

Do you know what happens if you take a twelve-week class designed to meet three times a week and squash it into a four-week class meeting four days a week? You end up with class sessions that are nearly three hours long but seem like thirty.

During the first hour I checked the roll and asked each student to tell the class where he or she was from and why they had signed up for Major Romantic Poets, and that managed to take up most of the hour. Several of them I knew from the previous summer—Don MacArthur, Karen Hix, Marian Slate, and, of course, Margaret Street.

I also opened my weekly calendar, made an appointment for each student to come talk with me about term paper topics, then gave the class a break. As they filed out toward the vending machines, I noticed how the room had already started to look more lived-in. I smiled at the disarranged chairs and the cluttered tables, the crumpled tissue dropped on the carpet. Out in the commons room they were already moving chairs around and leaving Coke can rings on the tables.

After the break I drew a deep breath and dove into Lecture #1.

"In a sense," I said, "all poets everywhere have always been romantics. Look at Virgil. . . ."

"There you are," I said nearly an hour later, pointing to the final item on the overhead projection. "Eleven essential characteristics of Romantic Period poetry, courtesy of Professor Ernest Bernbaum. I've placed his book, *Guide Through the Romantic Movement*, on reserve in the library. Please review these characteristics before our next class meeting and find examples in your textbook.

"Those of you who don't yet have a term paper topic might consider narrowing one of these eleven characteristics into a manageable research topic. For example, Mister MacArthur told me during break he's interested in the Romantics' fascination with the Gothic and the macabre. He could . . . and I offer this just as an illustration of what I mean by narrowing a topic . . . he could search through the poetry to see how our poets used allusion in creating their Gothic settings. Keats, for example, wrote a poem called 'The Eve of Saint Agnes' and in it he made an allusion to an old medieval poem called '*La belle dame sans merci*'. To those who know '*La belle dame*' the allusion adds a note of fright, you see. It's as if I were describing your daughter's first prom and mentioned that her escort had two long front teeth and wore a cape. My allusion to Stoker's famous vampire would be frightening enough even though I have not mentioned vampires directly."

"Professor McIntyre?"

"Yes, Miz . . . uh, Bronnick?"

"I was thinking maybe, when the Romantic poets were interested in Gothic and macabre subjects, it was because they felt isolated. Do you know what I mean? I mean, maybe they were young and idealistic and felt misunderstood or cut off from their society, so they liked these topics that would shock the establishment. Would that make a good paper do you think?"

"That would depend on your argument and your examples. But let's talk about it in class tomorrow. Meanwhile, see if you can think of ways to narrow it down, maybe to one poet or one set of poems. OK? Other questions?"

I paused and looked around for raised hands or inquiring looks or any sign at all that the students wanted me to continue talking. What I got instead was a collection of faces frozen into immobility, breathless with dread that someone else might ask a question. I decided they had suffered enough for the first class.

"Well," I said, looking at my watch, "let's call it an early day. Don't forget your conference appointments with me, and do read the assignment before tomorrow."

My first office conference was with one of the veterans of last summer's class in novels named for heroines.

"So . . . ," I began, sneaking a look at my appointment sheet to jog the professorial memory. As I always say to students, I can't remember faces but I always forget names. ". . . Miss Slate. Back for a second go at it, eh?"

"I was so glad when I heard they got you back again, Professor!"

I could have corrected her use of "got", except that (a) I use it that way myself, and (b) she was pretty, young, and glad to see me. Glad to see me always earns extra points.

"I wasn't that hard to get." I grinned. "Always need the money."

She made a chubby-lipped pout and a pooh-pooh sound as if it were general knowledge that my few books make as much money as Stephen King's. I only teach summers in Nebraska because I love to sweat, of course.

"Well, we are so glad to have you!" she puffed. She was a young teacher who already had the habit of talking to everyone the way she talks to her fifth graders. "There are several of us who signed up this summer just because it was you."

"Including Margaret Street," I observed.

"Didn't she drop out last summer?" Marian Slate asked.

"Along with two others. And Miss Deering . . . except that she didn't officially drop the class through the registrar. She was still on the rolls at the end of the term."

It was a classic *faux pas*. As soon as the missing woman's name popped out of my mouth, I remembered that she and Marian Slate seemed to be close friends. I found myself amazed at having brought Cass Deering's name into this particular conversation.

This kind of thing had happened before. It's a pattern all too familiar to me. Consciously or unconsciously I dropped a name I hoped would lead to a conversation about what had happened to the missing woman. By intention or by habit or by whatever, I obviously wanted to be involved with the problem of the Deering disappearance.

The problem. That's how I saw it—as a problem to be worked out. *The Rev. Walter W. Skeat's Etymological Dictionary of the English Language* tells us that the word "problem" comes from a Greek word meaning "to throw forward" or "to cast". That was me, all right, always casting about to see what I could come up with.

The real problem, maybe, is I can't see a puzzle without getting involved in it. I already knew that for the next four weeks Cass Deering's whereabouts could be the first thing on my mind every morning. There was a saving point, however: while she had been enrolled in my literature class, the fact that she was missing had nothing to do with books and literature. I mean this wasn't a case of a missing manuscript or an author leaving clues to hidden treasure. It didn't involve a rare edition or a fictional character that turned out to be an actual person. These are the kinds of puzzles likely to send me traipsing around and casting about after answers. But if a puzzle wasn't connected to literature, I could generally just let it go.

Miss Slate seemed to be listening to my thoughts. "Well, I guess I should tell you that she didn't stop coming to class because of anything you said. It had nothing to do with the class. It's just that she was having these serious problems and lost interest in everything else. And then right after the class ended there was the murder . . . oh, if only we would hear something!"

The flesh of her soft cheeks was already drawing up to receive the generous tears just beginning to glisten in her eyes.

"How she could just go away like that," she went on, "with none of her things, nothing!"

"Well," I said in my best soothing tone, "I'm sure someone will hear from her when she's ready to tell you where she is. I'll bet she'll come driving right into town one day. Let's not worry about it right now, OK?" I drew a yellow pad toward me and uncapped my pen. "Let's hear your ideas for a paper about one of our poets. Did you have a chance to read any of them before the summer session?"

"That's the other thing," Miss Slate said, putting a tissue to her eyes to staunch the overflow. "Those books she gave away."

"Books?" I said. *Oh, damn,* I thought. *Here we go. . . .*

"Well,"—she sniffed bravely and copiously—"well, I think I was first. Last summer she told me she wrote to you for the reading list."

"I remember," I said. "I was impressed by her initiative. That was, I think, before Christmas, maybe Thanksgiving. I didn't even know what the exact list would be, at that point, so I sent her a tentative one. *Daisy Miller*, *Jane Eyre*, *My Ántonia*, *Emma*, I think. *Madame Bovary* and *Lolita* and *Moll Flanders*. I can't recall the others on that list. She wanted to read them before the term started, or at least that's what her letter said."

"And she did, too!"

"But that's not unheard of," I said. "Every once in a while I have an eager student who gets a syllabus and reads the stuff before class even starts." Gets. Stuff. Now it was I who was mangling the Queen's diction.

"Yes, but Cass bought extra copies. Fresh new ones. And gave them to people."

"But I've done that myself," I said. "I often give books to people I like. I mean I give books I like to people. I like the people, too." Miss Slate was affecting my synapses as well as my syntax.

"With her it was different, though," she said. Her eyes took on a faraway look as though she were looking into a well of pain and loneliness. She no longer seemed to be in the office with me.

"Miss Slate?" I said at last.

"*Hmm?*" She came back, but slowly. "Oh, sorry! I was just thinking whether I could tell you. I mean you don't live around here, so it might be all right. Just in general terms, maybe. Do you remember what happens in *Jane Eyre*?"

"Yes," I said, without pointing out that I had taught the book.

"About Jane and Mister Rochester?"

"You mean how she falls in love with him and is going to marry him, and then discovers he's already married to the crazy woman he keeps in the attic?"

"Yes, that's it."

"Go on."

"It's just that I was in what you might call a parallel situation. Sort of. I mean . . . well . . . there was . . . a man. He hired me to help him home school his children. One thing led to another, and . . . well, you know. From what he told me, I thought he was a widower, but later on, after it was too late, I found out he was married and his wife had cancer. She was being treated in a hospital in another state. He'd go to see her and she didn't remember who he was and he knew she would never leave that place. He needed someone . . . he needed me But he still was married. Do you see what I'm saying?"

I knew I was seeing a very real, very romantic, very painful complex of emotions behind the pretty round face. I wasn't ready to deal with it.

"I'm sorry," I said, "but I really don't think I want to hear. . . ."

"Cass gave me a copy of *Jane Eyre*, and in it she marked places that related directly to me. She wrote notes to me in the margins. She stuck yellow sticky notes in places so I'd be sure to read a certain part. Professor, it was so weird how Jane Eyre's feelings were like mine. It was like Brontë had used me in the novel. And inside the back cover Cass wrote me a long note all about how things would be OK, and true love was strong, and I had to understand him like Jane understood Mister Rochester."

I leaned back, embarrassed at hearing a student's confession of an affair. But I realized that I was also relieved at the same time: the "literary connection" between Cass Deering's disappearance and the summer reading list was not of much consequence.

"And she did the same with three others. At least that I know of."

"What?"

"She did the same with three others. Three friends of hers who could have been in those novels. She gave them each a book with notes in it explaining connections. It was a long time before I found out about the other ones, because it's not the kind of thing you want to talk about in a small town, especially if you're teaching in the public school system."

"I guess not," I said. "Still. . . ."

"The girl she gave *Lolita* to was the worst, I guess. I won't tell you what her name is because I promised her. She's a grown woman now, but years ago, when she was thirteen or fourteen, she ran away from home and took a long road trip with an older man. He worked here in town, then he left. Last summer he showed up again after all those years and wanted to take up with her again. Let me tell you, she was suicidal. But Cass talked to her. And then later on she told me Cass gave her a copy of *Lolita* and helped her get things in perspective. Cass has a way . . . how can I say it . . . she has a way of understanding people, what makes them tick. She's not always right, of course, but just having someone care can really matter."

"Wait a minute," I said. "You seem to be saying that Cass . . . Miss Deering . . . told you things you didn't tell the police. You and this other woman, the one with the *Lolita* experience, might have some helpful information."

"Oh! Please, Professor McIntyre, please don't tell the police any of this! It's such a small town. So many people could get hurt."

"But Miss Deering. . . ."

"All I'm saying is Cass saw herself as one of the people

31

in those books. That's my point. A couple of times she said things, things that I didn't think meant much, until I started finding out about these other friends and the books she gave them. I just wonder, that's all. It just makes me wonder. I mean what if she read about a woman who killed her lover and threw herself into the sea or something?"

"We're in Nebraska," I said, trying to lighten up the conversation.

"Down a well, then . . . or climb up and jump into a grain elevator. You could smother in an elevator full of wheat. Or there are plenty of old gravel pits around here. Or remember that man in Willa Cather's novel, the one who dived headfirst into the grain separator or thresher or whatever it was?"

"Miss Slate," I said carefully, "you know her much better than I did, but I don't see her as the kind of person who'd kill herself on the spur of the moment. No note, no preparations, nothing."

Marian Slate sniffed and dried her eyes, and we managed to get back to the subject of her term paper. After she left, I found myself staring out the window and thinking about what she had said. What would Sergeant Houghton say if I took him a copy of *My Ántonia* and told him: "Look, Bob, Cass read this novel where a man jumps into a threshing machine and kills himself, so you need to search all the grain elevators and threshing machines in the county"?

My walk back to the trailer late that afternoon was clouded in black thoughts. In choosing this particular set of novels named for heroines, had I unknowingly wandered into some kind of *terra incognita* of the feminine psyche? Could the emotional sympathy between women actually extend to fictional characters that are female? Did my reading list somehow create an emotional bond between a living, breathing, suffering soul and one straight out of the pages of fiction? What if that contact had led to homicide or suicide? Or both?

My bag of books and papers were heavy, and my feet seemed to drag along the hot sidewalks and across the soft, tacky tar of the streets. Talk about Gothic—I felt like Byron's outcast or Coleridge's ancient mariner, spreading gloom like the shadow of dark wings. It was clear, after talking to Marian Slate, that Cass Deering had seen her friends' problems in a collection of novels that were of my choosing. And if one of those same novels was somehow connected to the murder and to her disappearance. . . .

Jane Dorner certainly knew what she was doing when it came to scheduling. According to Board of Education rules, we needed six contact hours of class per week, so she suggested having the class meet from seven to ten in the morning on Mondays and Wednesdays, eight to ten on Fridays, and one conference hour per week. The only problem was that it shut out the working people who couldn't get their workday rearranged for those four weeks. But then, again, how many working people need to take an advanced class in Romantic Period poetry?

The seven in the morning thing was the best. If I could get up by five in the morning and out of the trailer by six, I would have the day's most beautiful hour in which to organize my thoughts and review my lecture plan while strolling to campus. At that hour, the prairie sun is fresh and welcome. You can catch the scent of dew on freshly turned flower beds. The shadows of old elm trees lie along the sidewalks. Cats who have been on dawn patrol will mew at you, but they don't stop to chat. They're on their way home for breakfast. Small birds pipe hymns to a world born anew with each sunrise.

There's a big quiet everywhere that makes you want to stand still and listen. And if you do, you hear the sounds of a town coming to life: a screen door slamming somewhere, a car starting up. You hear small feet and claws moving along the branches of the green sun-dappled canopy overhead. A boy on a bicycle passes you on his way to somewhere and it's so quiet you're aware of the hum of his tires and the click-clatter of the bicycle chain.

Ms. Dorner's schedule also got me out of the classroom by ten or ten-thirty, just as the prairie sun was beginning to lay full siege to our bastion of learning, turning the open lawns and sidewalks seriously warm. But at ten-thirty or eleven, provided I didn't have to stay around for student conferences, I could sling my canvas bag of notes, books, and papers over my shoulder and walk down to Houghton's Hut. I always looked forward to pushing open the door and feeling the first blast of chilled air and inhaling the aroma of café coffee.

On Friday, Sergeant Bob Houghton was already sitting at the table next to the window, keeping an eye on Central Street while nursing his second cup of coffee. I took the chair on the other side of the table. Our conversation began with the weather, went into how my job was going and how his was going, and eventually came around to the Deering case.

"So you haven't had a lead in what, two months? Three?" I asked.

The sergeant of police counted on his fingers—after licking the powdered sugar from the index finger. Betty allowed him one donut per day, period. "Let's see. Second week of August the murder was. Then September. Heard a few things this spring, in May. In June, not much. What's this, the last week in July? Yep, two months or better."

"What did you hear in September?" I asked. "Was it about her, or about the victim?"

"Her, kind of. There's a little mom 'n' pop motel out on the edge of town . . . maybe you've seen it . . . and the woman says she rented a room to a skinny fella with receding hair and bad complexion, like he'd been sick or on drugs she thought. A couple of weeks after the murder happened, she finally came in and told us she thought it was Cass Deering's husband."

"Husband?" I said. "I didn't think she had a husband."

"Neither did anyone else. She said he looked kind of like somebody she'd seen with Cass a year ago . . . maybe more . . . but he'd changed. A lot. Like he'd been really sick. Anyway, this stranger said he was in town to 'find his wife'. And he kind of smiled real sad, she said, like it meant he was looking for a wife. You know, just hoping to meet some woman he could marry. But the next day he asked the woman's husband if he knew where Cass Deering lived."

"So what happened to him?" I asked, the old surge of curiosity rising again. A strange man coming to a small town looking for a woman he once knew or a woman he once married. It had a familiar ring to it, like something I had read somewhere. That's another one of my problems: too much reading, and too many "somewheres".

"Ah," Houghton said, poking the last little chunk of his powdered donut into his mouth, "that's part of the problem! Mystery, I guess you could say. Left the same day the murder happened. And he didn't pay his bill for that night."

"Did he leave anything behind?" I asked, wishing I didn't care.

"Toothbrush and one of those little tubes of toothpaste. A plastic disposable razor in the bathroom. Don't you hate those dumb things? I'll take a good ol' Gillette any day. Not that you use one, Doc," and he stroked at his clean chin while eyeing my close-trimmed salt-and-pepper beard.

"That's it? A guy staying in a motel and doesn't leave anything behind?"

"There was a prescription bottle with two pills in it, setting on the sink, like so he'd remember to take them later. The Greyhound driver said the guy got off the bus carrying one bag, one of those carry-on size things, and I guess he left town with it. The other stuff, it was like he packed and left in a hurry and just forgot to look in the bathroom. Y'ever do that?"

"No, but I've left socks and underwear in motel dressers before. What were the pills?" I said.

"John down at the pharmacy says they're a generic pill for internal parasites, like you might get in a hot climate where there isn't any sanitation. They came from one of those big chain drug stores in Denver. Name of the customer was Michael Whyte, but they didn't have an address. Transient apparently. A walk-in clinic in New York wrote the prescription."

"Fingerprints?"

"Not really. The woman cleaned the room to a fare-thee-well. And she handled the toothbrush and razor. Put 'em in a sack, in case he came back, along with the pills. It finally occurred to her, too late, there might be a connection to the Deering case."

Houghton pushed his cup toward the edge of the table as the waitress came by, and smiled at her as she filled it up. She looked at me with an inquiring eyebrow, but I put my hand over my cup.

"No, thanks," I told her. But I wasn't ready to leave the Hut just yet.

"What's this marriage thing about?" I asked. "Anybody know about a husband?"

"Can't say," Houghton said. "One of my guys phoned around to county offices in the state, but came up dry. Some little counties, here and in Kansas, Colorado, Wyoming, they just take the money, maybe look at a blood test and birth certificate, but they don't always get around to recording a marriage. A marriage certificate could go into some clerk's stack of stuff and stay there for months. And that's if they were really married legally. Maybe she didn't use her right name, maybe they got hitched in some off-beat church somewhere."

"How did he register at the motel?"

"Michael Whyte. But how many times have you checked into a motel with a phony name?"

I actually started to think if I could remember a time, then realized Houghton was kidding. His grin looked like one of those yellow smiley stickers.

"All the time," I said. "You know my reputation."

"I know enough of it," he said.

Back outside, I felt the Nebraska summer heat hit my back like somebody was ironing my shirt while I was still wearing it. The shade under the arching trees was no longer cool and moist, but now trapped the hot air like an oven. As I walked along, I thought about the trailer and wished I had left the air conditioning turned on.

I walked by houses and apartments where shades were drawn shut and thought about all the invisible people in those places. How many people were in those houses waiting for other people to come home, and how many were glad and how many didn't care any more? How many of them waited for people who no longer came? In all the private emotions growing and living and dying behind those walls there was so much potential for loneliness, I thought. And loneliness, shared at some time or another by every human being who lives, is only one of many emotions, one small part of the microcosm of all human feelings, all human experience. All of it could be held in a single human soul, or contained behind the curtained windows of sidewalk houses in one small prairie town.

Chapter Three

Whither fled Lamia?
"Lamia"
—John Keats

"So, here's young John Keats at age twenty-three," I said, winding up my lecture, "writing about his fear that he may die before he can write all the poems swirling around in his brain. But when he suddenly thinks about never seeing his friend again, he becomes so unbearably lonely that fame means nothing to him. Now, to me . . . and you can argue with this if you want to . . . Keats seems to sum up the fundamental problem with the Romantics' idea of individualism, namely that it can get lonely. Our Romantic poets took pride in their individualistic thought, in separating themselves from 'crass' society, in finding unconventional religious beliefs, in believing themselves to be more 'sensitive' and more emotional than ordinary people. At the same time, like Keats, they frequently bemoaned their own isolation.

"OK. Let's quit on that happy thought, and perhaps one or two of you will have more to say about it after reading the next assignment. So, same time, same place, same book next class."

As the students packed up and shuffled out of the room, I almost felt like running after them and suggesting we all go to the Homesteader for a beer. I was glad the school day was over, but, like John Keats, I wasn't ready to be alone. I shrugged it off, though; it was just the intensity of the summer session starting to show up. When you squash a full sixteen-week semester into sixteen sessions, it makes each day feel more like a week. It was only Wednesday afternoon of the second week and I already needed a vacation, or at least a change of pace. I walked back to the Prairie View Trailer Park picturing a bottle of cold beer I had in the refrigerator. All I wanted to do was sit in front of the air conditioner vent and have a drink. But that was before I got to the trailer and saw poor old Horse sitting there in the full sun with heat waves coming off his hood like he was a slab of steak under a broiler. It was my fault for not parking under the elm tree the night before.

I tossed my canvas briefcase into the trailer and went back outside. I was tempted to spit on my finger and touch it to Horse's front fender, the way my mother used to do to see if the electric iron was hot.

"How would you like to take a little run to cool off?" I asked him. "Maybe we'll stop for a beer on the way back."

Even with the windows down the steel cab was like a sauna. I put my back against the Naugahyde an inch at a time to ease the shock of hot plastic hitting a sweaty shirt. Four pumps of the gas pedal and a turn of the key and 318 cubic inches came to life with a roar people probably heard clear across town. I turned the fan to "HI" but the air from the vents was as hot or hotter than the air in the cab.

Horse politely rumbled down the tree-lined streets of town, got more restless as we turned onto the wide two-lane highway, and after a couple of minutes on the smooth asphalt he got downright impatient. While I was still taking off my necktie and putting on my sunglasses, the old Dodge managed to sneak the speedometer up to seventy. Away we went toward the next little town on the map, Poplar Bend, the breeze blowing in the windows to stir up the dust on the floorboards, the radio playing oldies I'd never heard of, the big tires humming on the concrete. Distance and speed. What more can a truck ask for? I relaxed and drove with one hand on the top of the wheel, wondering whether Cass Deerfield had taken off down this road on the night her lover was murdered. Only three main roads run out of Alliance, so there was a good chance she used the same one I was now on.

The novels named after their heroines came to mind; each one seems to have a scene where the woman is going down a road, sooner or later. There's Ántonia, for example, in Cather's novel, leaving the scene of her shame, pregnant and going home to her people. Or Moll Flanders, tricked into joining her seducer in his carriage, is whisked away along country roads to his lair.

By the time we reached the sign marking the turn-off to Poplar Bend, I was cooled down and wind-ruffled and Horse seemed to have blown the cobs out of his engine. We took the turn-off, made a U-turn at a farm road, and dutifully stopped at the state's stop sign even though the view from horizon to horizon was uninterrupted by any kind of vehicle from tractors to tricycles. Then we accelerated back onto the highway and headed back toward that frosty beer.

A mile from Alliance, maybe more, Horse overtook one of those mini-size pickups. You know the kind. Made in Japan with a little four-pot engine that has less horsepower than Aunt Tillie's electric wheelchair? This particular one seemed to be slowing down, doing about fifty with two wheels on the hard shoulder. As I got closer, it was down to forty and I could see the guy had his right hand clapped to the side of his head, which meant either that he was using a damned cell phone or a wasp had flown into his ear. No wonder he was half off the road. I assumed he was slowing down so he could pull over to finish his phone call.

I looked in my mirrors, hit the signal lever, and pulled out around him. And just about at that point, wouldn't you know it, there was the highway sign marking the Alliance turn-off. It was going to be close. Making sure I could see all of his little toy truck in my right-hand mirror, I hit the accelerator pedal and gave Horse's eight cylinders and twin carburetors all the gas they could take. When I looked in the mirror again, I saw the driver now had his left hand out the window. He seemed to be sending me a message. Evidently my maneuver had annoyed him and in response he caught up and tailgated us for the next mile, all the way to the edge of town. He stuck to Horse's rear end like glue.

"Good idea, dummy," I said. "My truck weighs twice as much as yours. The steel in that rear bumper is like battleship armor. If I slam on my brakes, you'll be sitting there, eating your steering wheel, and your radiator will be in your lap."

He may have suddenly noticed how my trailer hitch lined up perfectly with the middle of his grill, or he may have just calmed down, but, whatever the reason, he dropped back and turned off down a side street. He flipped me the finger again in parting.

You, too, Charlie, I thought. *Next time hang up and drive.* I guess I should have felt a little guilty, cutting in like that, even though there was never any danger in it. But within a few blocks I was relaxed again and ready for that beer.

"Hey!" the bartender boomed when he saw me taking a stool in the semi-gloom down the bar. "Good to see you again! Still drinkin' the Budweisers?"

Ed's right hand was on the Bud tap while his left hand

tipped a chilled mug under it. Like all bartenders worth their margarita salt, he rarely forgot a person's face or a customer's favorite poison.

I sipped at the foam, savoring the anticipation of ice-cold lager sliding over the tongue.

"Ahhh," I said after a big swallow. "It's good to be back, Ed."

On a hot July afternoon, a Nebraska small town saloon is more than just a neighborhood business. It's a local refuge, a place to hide. But the people in the bar are not hiding from the hustle and bustle and tension of the town, because there isn't much. At least not much that you can readily see. No, the place is a sanctuary from the sun, that huge hot sun that seems to have stalled to a stop just after midday, hovering straight overhead as if lying in wait for victims.

On days such as this, people stop work on their flower beds and sit on the porch swing instead. Then they find the porch too hot and the sky full of glare, so they slip into the house hoping to find something down in the basement that needs doing. Laundry to fold, something. Anything, as long as it's out of the heat. Pretty soon you hear the low whine of the air conditioner coming on and you know they gave in. They'd rather face the electric bill than the sun's heat.

A saloon like Ed's is a cool grotto. It smells of working man's beer and cigarette smoke. There are clean smells, too, the piney scent of the stuff they use to oil the wood floor and the faint chlorine aroma from the sink behind the bar where Ed seems to be perpetually involved in swabbing out beer glasses.

My stool was under a ceiling fan turning slowly and silently. Murmurs of conversation came from the two booths in the back, and Ed's radio was turned down so low I couldn't tell if it was playing the Country Western station or the one with the golden oldies. It just hummed behind him as he swabbed glasses.

"Good winter?" Ed asked. I had been a regular customer last summer, stopping in his place two or three times a week for a cold Bud, but now he was fishing around for clues to remind him who I was and why I was back.

"Oh, you know," I said. "Nothing special. My classes were too full and the students didn't work hard enough and the faculty meetings were boring. I was glad to get back here where I can just teach a few adults and do my own thing."

"But it must be pretty quiet for you around here," he ventured, "after all that big city excitement in, uh. . . ."

"Boulder," I said. "University of Colorado. Tell you the truth, Ed, I don't take part in most of the big city excitement. I like things peaceful, like around here. Hey! I *did* hear Alliance had a murder this spring."

"You bet. Carl Deerfield. Somebody went and stabbed him with a butcher knife, right over there at Missus Samuels's place."

"No kidding. I stayed there last summer, you know."

"That's right," Ed said, realization spreading over his face. "Oh, sure. You taught a class at the college. 'Doc' something. Don't tell me, now. Boy, the brain really develops memory leaks after you get to fifty. Don't it? Ah! Got it! McIntyre."

I reached across the bar and shook hands with him as if we'd just been introduced.

"Dave McIntyre," I said. "And don't feel bad. I always forget names. But it works out pretty well, since I can't remember faces."

He didn't get it.

"So, you said his name was Carl Deerfield? It wasn't

Deering, was it? Cass Deering was in my class last summer."

"Nope, it was Deerfield." And as soon as Ed said that, I remembered that it was the name Bob Houghton had mentioned on the phone last winter. The similarity hadn't struck me until now.

"He came in a few times," Ed went on. "Can't really say I liked him much. When you talked to him, he seemed to look right past you. Seemed to just want to talk about himself, you know? Always gave me a strange feeling that he wanted something, but didn't want to say what it was. Ever know anybody like that? Anyway, he always made me feel on edge, like I needed to watch what I said. Had a kinda superior attitude, you might say."

"I know the type. You don't ever know quite how to talk to them."

A customer came in and took a seat two stools down.

" 'Scuse me a second," Ed said, wiping his hands.

"Sure," I said. The new arrival was a sullen-looking kid of medium height but skinny, and, in spite of looking like he couldn't punch his way out of a cardboard outhouse, he sported a couple of tattoos and ear jewelry like he thought he was a street fighter. One tattoo was a dragon on the upper arm, one of those dopey-looking lizards you pick out of a catalog at the needle parlor. The other one was a blurry strip around his wrist that was supposed to look like barbwire or a crown of thorns or something. The kind high school girls get on their ankles when they run out of other ways to attract unwanted attention. The kid had a mean, pissed-off look permanently etched into his face. Between the buzz cut hair with long fringes over the collar and the wispy wanna-be mustache there seemed to be nothing but blackheads, acne, and ego.

He ordered a beer and a shot of whiskey, just like a real man. He glared down the bar at me.

"That'd be your Dodge out there, wouldn't it," he growled into his shot glass.

" 'Seventy-Eight Camper Special," I said. "Three-quarter ton." And right away I knew he was the kid with the little toy pickup, the one I cut off on the highway.

"Somethin' wrong?" Ed inquired. The kid ignored me and talked to Ed.

"Damn' greenie tried to run me off the road a while ago, that's all," he muttered into his beer mug. In neighboring states, Coloradoans are sometimes called "greenies" because of the green license plates. It's not a term of endearment.

The kid found his courage and stood up, glaring at me, gripping his nearly empty beer mug like a weapon. I got my foot on the floor and looked around for a stick of some description, like a broom or mop. Ed reached behind the bar and brought out a six-foot metal tube with a loop of wire on one end, used for catching stray dogs and raccoons. Besides being a volunteer fireman, Ed is also the town's volunteer deputy animal control officer. He put the catchpole on the bar.

"Gonna hit me with that?" the kid snarled.

"No," Ed said calmly. "I'm gonna give it to Doc here and he's gonna use it to toss you out into the street. Doc does that martial arts thing with sticks, you know. What do y' call it, Doc?" Ed had started to remember me pretty well.

"*Bojutsu,*" I said, placing my hand on the bar just inches from the catchpole.

The kid thought it over while he studied my face. Dumb as he looked, he still had to notice I had some advantages including the metal pole, thirty pounds of body weight, and one bartender. He set the beer mug down. Maybe he wasn't as dumb as he looked.

Never one to want his stools and windows broken in a brawl, Ed started to apply some of the barroom diplomacy he has picked up over the years. "Doc, here," he said as if he was just continuing a conversation, "was telling me he had a collection of *Playboy* magazines goin' back to the first issue."

"No kiddin'," said the twerp. "I'd like to see that." He was still surly, but he took this chance to back out of a tight situation.

"Yeah," I said, "too bad it's back in Colorado. I'd let you look through it."

"Too bad," he said, returning to his beer.

Where Ed got the idea of telling the kid I owned a *Playboy* collection I'll never know, but I could see he knew his clients and how to distract them. This particular one, known locally as Ronnie Webber, was an inveterate girl ogler. He had progressed from juvenile peeping-tom to teen voyeur, and then to horny young adult. If he managed to live past fifty, he'd be promoted to lecher.

Ed drew me another beer and took my glass so he'd have something to wash and polish. "So," he continued, "this Deerfield character never seemed to fit in around here. I guess he lived with his mother on a farm somewhere west of town. Then somehow he got an idea to be one of them what-do-you call 'em . . . sort of a preacher."

"Evangelist?" I ventured.

"No, more into that motivational stuff. He traveled around the state with a bunch of posters and brochures advertising himself as a speaker and consultant."

"Like an inspirational speaker, you mean."

"Yeah. That, and something he called 'life coaching' or

something. It didn't work out, obviously. He came back here and pretty soon he was living with Cass Deering in that room Missus Samuels has over her garage. Didn't you stay there last summer?"

"I had the other room, the one upstairs in the back of her house."

"Oh, yeah. Well, he's dead now. Her, too, probably. My own guess is some other woman broke into the apartment and stabbed him, and Cass tried to pull the butcher knife out of him . . . that's how she got her fingerprints on it . . . and then this woman grabbed her or made her leave at gun-point and took her out of town in her own car and killed her. At least that's what I'd like to think happened, even if it does seem kinda far-fetched."

Ronnie Webber shoved his empty beer mug down the bar toward Ed and followed it by moving to the stool next to mine.

"Had a 'Eighty-Nine Ford Fairlane," he said abruptly. "Kind of a silver blue four door."

"How's that?" I asked.

"That's her car. It's a 'Eighty-Nine Ford Fairlane."

"Ronnie, here," Ed explained, "probably knows more about cars than most men in town. At least he knows every car in this town."

"But she ain't dead," Ronnie said. "I seen her two weeks ago over in Morris. Seen that car, too, or one just like it, sittin' right there at the Reddy-Credit Auto Sales."

"What do you mean, you *saw* her?" Ed said. "Did you tell Sergeant Houghton?"

"Hell, Houghton don't know nuthin'," Ronnie said. "I don't talk to that bastard."

Let me guess, I thought as I gave Ronnie the once-over. *Here we have a living road hazard that likes cars and speed, spies on women, drinks whiskey with his beer in mid-afternoon, and sports tattoos and earrings. My guess is that Houghton had gotten into Ronnie's face more than once.*

"So where'd you say you saw her?"

"Ah, I went down to Morris a couple of weeks ago. There's nothin' to do in this damn' town."

"So," Ed said. "You went down there to the Bootstrap Club to watch those girls dance on tables, didn't you?"

"So what?" Ronnie replied. "At least they're good-lookin', not like the ones around here."

"And you saw Cass Deering there," I prompted.

"If it ain't her, it's her twin sister. She's dancin' there. I thought . . . 'how come none of the other guys from here ever recognized her?' . . . and then I figured it was the lighting and the make-up, or something. Besides, most guys would hardly look at her face. She's got a set of. . . ."

"Never mind," Ed said. "You better let Houghton know about this."

"Screw Houghton," Ronnie said. "He's so smart, let him figure it out. You know what? I think I saw 'em leave the night that guy was stabbed, only I never told Houghton. Wouldn't give him the satisfaction."

"Saw who?"

"You know where my place is," Ronnie said to Ed. Then he looked at me. "I got the rooms over Anderson's garage next door t'old Missus Samuels. I hear everything that goes on in that apartment of hers."

"And?" Ed said.

"That night they woke me up, arguing like hell over there. About midnight, when I was just about to get to sleep, somebody slammed a door, real hard. Then about three a.m. or three-thirty, they were yellin' at each other and finally there's this kind of scream or a groan like a man does when you kick him in the groin. It got real quiet then, and I was just about asleep again when they started up that Ford. I looked out and seen it drive off down the alley."

"Well, Jesus, Ronnie," Ed exclaimed, "you should have told Houghton all this! Dammit, man, that's important! It was a murder, after all."

"None of my business," Ronnie sniffed. "Houghton already accused me of peekin' in people's windows. I don't wanna be dragged off and questioned for no forty-eight hours, neither. Anyway, if he wants her, all he has to do is drive to Morris."

Ed was on the phone to the police station.

"Penny?" he said. "How y'doin'? This is Ed over at the Homesteader. Oh, pretty good. Say, is Bob there? Oh. Well, if you can get him on the radio, you might tell him to come over here. No, no trouble. But there's something about the Deering case he needs to know. OK. Thanks. 'Bye."

Ronnie Webber made a show out of tossing off the rest of his whiskey, although the glass had long since gone dry, and hitched his jeans up around his scrawny hips.

"If that son-of-a-bitch is on his way over here, I'm leavin'."

"You better wait around. He'll want to talk to you."

"He never has no trouble findin' me. I got things to do."

We watched Ronnie hurry out into the dazzling sun. Ed offered to draw me another beer, but I, too, had things I needed to do. I wanted to wait around for Houghton, but I didn't need to be fuzzy-headed the rest of the day.

"Where does that kid work?" I asked.

"Oh, anywhere," Ed said. "He's a pretty fair mechanic, so long as it doesn't involve computers. He's worked at the gas station, Dale's garage, the Allis-Chalmer dealership. Right now I think he's driving the tow truck for Dale. Always talking about either cars or women. And usually"—Ed smiled—"usually he'll tell you all about his plans to get himself a really good one as soon as he has the money."

"Car, or a woman?"

"You got it." Ed grinned.

"Now tell me more about this *Playboy* collection of mine."

Sergeant Houghton came in within ten minutes, looking at Ed with a knowing smirk on his face.

"You look like a man with a friendly hamster in his pocket," Ed said.

"I've been grinning about *you,* you backward redneck." Houghton laughed. "Telling Penny to see if she could get me on the radio. Where you been, boy? Never seen one of these?" Houghton unclipped the pager from his belt and showed Ed the display screen. When he put it back on the belt, he touched the holster holding his cell phone. " 'Try to get him on the radio.' " He laughed. "Boy, that's a good one. She can page me or phone me anywhere, even when I'm in the john. So, what's up?"

Between the two of us, we filled Houghton in on what Ronnie had said about the girl dancing at the strip club in Morris and about the car in the lot. Houghton sat on a stool, calmly eating pretzels and listening until we had exhausted our information. And I don't know about Ed, but I was excited as a schoolboy tattling to the teacher about who put the super glue on the toilet seats.

Sergeant Houghton listened with patience before he tossed cold water on us.

"Boys," he said, "I sure appreciate your wanting to help with the police work. But I have to tell you, I already know about that car and the girl in Morris. The car isn't Cass's.

51

The week she vanished, we called around to all the car lots in the county, and the junkyards, and they put the description of her car on their Internet. They exchange information on what cars and parts are available and where. That Ford in Morris showed up on the computer, but it isn't hers. Same year and model, but not hers."

"And the stripper?" I asked.

"First off, she's not exactly a stripper. I mean, she *does* strip, but she's what is called an exotic dancer. Pretty good at it, too. Nothing cheap about her. Classy, I guess you could say. I didn't spread it around because she asked me not to, but she turns out to be Cass Deering's sister. Looks a lot like her. But I went down to Morris, talked with her, and got her statement and all that, and I've called her a couple of times since. She's as clueless as we are about what happened to her sister."

So much for amateur enthusiasm. Still, as I left the bar and fired up Horse to go to the grocery and then back to the trailer, I couldn't get over the idea that this sister might know something. Something she doesn't know she knows, maybe. Or something she doesn't want anyone to know.

Chapter Four

This riddling tale, to what does it belong?
Is't history? vision? or an idle song?
"Phantom or Fact"
—Samuel Taylor Coleridge

T. S. Eliot knew what he was talking about. "There will be time," he wrote, "time to prepare a face to meet the faces that you meet." I lift my hand to open a classroom door and prepare my face.

The varnished door swung open with a soft whooshing sound as if the classroom had been hermetically sealed. The fluorescent lights with their chrome diffusers spread an eerily even illumination over the light gray Formica tables at which the students were already seated. It all seemed so formal, so expectant.

Well, I thought, let's see who's missing today. Talk about mystery and suspense—will Margaret be here today? Has she dropped class again? Did she read any of the assignment? Did anyone read the assignment?

The mystery wasn't Margaret, however, but the surprise visitor. She was sitting at the end of the right-hand table, facing me. The moment I plopped my bag down on the table, I knew who she was. But what the heck was she doing here?

Do you know those glossy hosiery catalogs you get in the mail, the ones showing a leggy brunette with her legs crossed at the ankle modeling the latest shade of sheer nylon? Or, there are the newspaper ads featuring shapely calves encased in such trendy hues as taupe, autumn smoke, misty tease, and take-no-prisoners.

Such legs actually exist. They are not just fantasies from some ad agent's overworked imagination. The proof was sitting in my classroom that morning, smiling up at me. A perfectly average woman—if you overlook the dimple-to-dimple smile, the modestly tailored summer suit, the hair impossibly perfect for seven in the morning, and those incredible legs. It was Professor Henriette Palmer of the CU Department of History. She is a colleague, sometime acts as a foil for my sharp and endearing wit, flirts without hesitation, is the envy of every co-ed, is unmarried, and, as far as I know, is irreproachably moral. Of the few women in my orbit who show genuine class, Professor Palmer is out in front.

I call her Hank, of course.

But what the hell was she doing in my 7:00 a.m. class 600 miles from our home university, dressed like a corporate lawyer, and smiling at me? I have been known to show up in her lectures, just to see if I could throw her off guard with a grin or an incredulous expression on my face at one of the points she was making. She's dropped in on my classes, too, but usually on days when she wants company for lunch and isn't picky about who she's seen with. But to drive 600 miles?

I took the roll, noticing that all and sundry were in attendance, including Margaret Street.

"And we have a visitor," I announced. "I'd like to introduce Professor Henriette Palmer from the CU Department of History. Professor, are you just traveling through Nebraska or have you accepted a new position here?"

Hank has a laugh . . . how can I put this? I'll just say that everyone turned to look when I introduced her, and those who had turned back to their books and notes looked back at her when they heard her voice. That kind of laugh. Soft. Genuine. Unique. Hearing it could make a man drop something on his foot and not feel it.

"Just passing through, I'm afraid," she said. "Naturally I couldn't pass up an opportunity to hear an authentic D. L. McIntyre lecture." The class enjoyed that one.

"Professor Palmer taught here two summers ago," I explained. "In fact, it was through her I got my job last summer. But, unfortunately for auld lang syne, we need to get down to work. Today I thought I would review one of Wordsworth's key points from the Preface to *Lyrical Ballads*, then ask each of you for an application of it to your weekend reading. After the break we'll circle up the chairs and chat about Coleridge."

I took my customary perch on the edge of the lecture table, spread my notes beside me, and began.

"While most readers are drawn to Wordsworth's theory about the process of poetry, the way in which a 'true' poem comes into being, there are important points concerning the object or purpose of poetry which are actually more important in understanding the scope and effect of the Romantic Movement. . . ."

For the next hour I doled out dollops of literary theory and history and the students offered up examples. They asked questions, to which I responded with my usual glittering wisdom. Break time finally arrived, and, over a can of Coke from the lounge, Hank explained that she was on her way back from a Western History Association committee session. Her trip home brought her within fifty miles of Alliance and she had a few days to spend, so she had just dropped in.

"Just to see how you are doing." She smiled. "Well . . . partly to see if you'd be surprised to see me sitting in your class! And I want to look up some friends."

"Let me guess," I said, eyeing her trim, professional appearance, "you have a ten o'clock appointment with the history chairman . . . what's his name."

"Harold Hunter. Only it's at ten-thirty. Some detective you are!" She beamed another smile using her eyes as well as her carefully glossed lips. Double jeopardy, I think it's called.

"So you won't be coming back into class after the break," I said.

"No. Your lecture is just lovely, but no. I did tell Hunter I'd meet him this morning."

I tossed my Coke can at the recycle barrel. It went off the rim and fell into the adjoining paper bin. Professor Palmer carefully dropped hers into the barrel, and then retrieved mine—with two fingers—and put it there as well.

"Staying in town tonight?" I said.

"I could. What's up?"

"Let's rustle up some kind of picnic food and go have a picnic," I suggested. "Evenings around here tend to get pretty long. What do you say? I'll show you something interesting, in fact. Ever been out to Carhenge?"

"Of course. Oh, I know what you mean . . . they have picnic tables out there. Lovely! I'll find a motel somewhere and pick you up. Where are you staying?"

"Oh, I can't afford a room anywhere. I just sleep in the back of Horse. Usually spend the night parked in front of whatever saloon I lurched out of."

"I believe it." She smiled. "You're the only professor eligible for senior discounts who actually likes to sleep in the back of a truck. *Eeeugh.*"

"Try the Prairie View Trailer Park then, whenever you're ready. Or the Homesteader bar. I need to get back to my eager pupils."

"Fair enough," she said. "I'll see you later, then."

It was true I needed to get back to my waiting students, but I wasn't in such a hurry that I couldn't pause to watch Hank walk away. What man wouldn't?

"Now," I said to start the second session, "let's open things up. Who found something in Coleridge that caught their attention? Just anything at all."

"Professor McIntyre?" It was Michelle Clairemont.

"Yes?"

"Would you go over 'Work Without Hope'? I'm not sure I got it."

"There's not much to get. It takes place in late February and the poet sees the birds beginning to mate, the bees are starting to move around, and nature in general is getting busy. But he doesn't have anything to do. Or I guess I should say he can't get to work because he has lost his hope of doing anything worthwhile. He can't find an object for hope, anything to hope for. Is that the part that seems vague to you?"

"Well . . . yes and no. Suppose you had a kind of ambition, you know? But everything you do turns out wrong. I mean you have this hope, but you give up working on it because it always goes wrong."

Vic Martley tried to come to her assistance.

"I think what Michelle is saying is that you just get tired of trying to accomplish something, you know? And didn't Coleridge use drugs?"

"That may or may not be relevant," I said. "In his twenties he was in love, desperately, but it was a hopeless love.

57

He had several physical ills, like rheumatism, and doctors gave him laudanum for the pain. That's opium dissolved in alcohol. There was a woman he couldn't have, and she married another man. Coleridge married another woman, but for the wrong reasons. Lots of pain and confusion. But this poem was written much later, after he found some peace and quiet. Let's go back to the question. Miss Clairemont?"

"*Hmm?*" she said, looking up with eyes on the verge of tears. "I don't know. I marked the phrase 'wreathless brow', what does that mean?"

"It means the poet has not achieved fame, hasn't earned his laurel wreath."

"Oh."

She fell silent. Among the other students and myself the conversation moved on into talk of disappointed love and from there into the poetic self-image, but Miss Clairemont was not with us. The hour eventually ended and she lingered until all the others had left the room and the door was closed.

"What's the matter?" I asked. "Your mind left the room before you did, if you know what I mean."

She knew. She was not an eighteen-year old college freshman, but a young mature woman, a teacher. I seemed to recall that she taught drama in Scottsbluff.

"I don't know," she said. "Something about saying hope without an object, I guess. I was thinking about Cass. You know . . . Cass Deering?"

"I remember," I said. "Sad situation."

"You see. . . ." She hesitated, took a deep breath, went on. "You see Cass was there for me . . . when I needed somebody to give me some perspective. Do you know the theatre term 'giving notes'?"

"Yes," I said. "I believe that's when a fellow actor or the

director reviews your performance and tells you what was good and bad about it."

"Mostly bad." She tried to smile. "Cass did that for me. There was a man . . . well, I won't get into all that. Let's just say he tried to convince me . . . he did convince me . . . I should try professional acting. He got me to go to Chicago with him. Oh, God, it was awful. Told me he wasn't married but he was."

I wasn't comfortable with this. I dug around in my briefcase for a stick of chewing gum, checked to see if I'd erased the board, anything to show embarrassment. She noticed, but her own impetus carried her on.

"He did get me acting jobs, but in really bad places. Then his wife showed up . . . God, this is like a soap opera . . . and took everything he had and left him. Then *he* had a breakdown with drugs and everything, and ended up in a halfway house. At least that's what I heard. I just had to get out of there."

"So, Cass . . . ," I said, steering her back to more neutral ground.

"Oh. See, Cass . . . I phoned her one night from Chicago and told her everything. A couple of days later she mailed me a copy of *Sister Carrie*. By Dreiser? That's how I ended up taking your class last summer."

"I don't follow."

"Cass underlined things in that book, and wrote sticky notes and stuck them on passages that sounded just like my life. 'See,' she told me, 'you aren't the first one. You just need to put it behind you.' And I didn't want to end up like Sister Carrie, so I got out of Chicago. And I was lucky . . . the school needed me back. But it seemed like I was giving up my hope, like Coleridge said. My hope of being a professional actress. But I was working without any hope.

Anyway, I came back here, and, if I could earn some summer credits, it would be like starting over, working toward a permanent teaching job."

I took up my bag and began to drift the both of us toward the door.

"So you're saying this novel Cass gave you really hit you," I said.

"It's hard to explain," she said. "You read about somebody so much like yourself and it's like you're in the book. It's scary! It's even scarier when somebody else sees the same similarity."

We went up the wide stairs and through the big doors and outside, where we parted company. But as I walked toward the trailer park, she was still on my mind. *Sister Carrie,* I thought. Did Cass Deering see *herself* in *Sister Carrie*? Or could it be scratched off the list as one more novel she didn't relate to? There are two men in that novel. One is the ego-driven Drouet and the other is Hurstwood, the phony husband. Not only that, I muttered to myself, not only that. Hurstwood steals money and hustles himself and Carrie off to Canada. Somebody hustled Cass off to somewhere after she killed Deerfield. Was there a parallel? I wondered.

There's an old stereotype of the absent-minded professor who is not only out to lunch but can't even remember *having* lunch. It is a state of mind caused by just such a situation as I was in, where the brain is performing a *postmortem* on the class session just ended, while trying at the same time to plan the next one. Some other part of the brain might be working on an idea for a book. On top of all that, my own gray cells were preoccupied with this growing puzzle, the conundrum of a missing woman who gave her friends books containing weird similarities to their lives.

It was also getting so warm outside I was debating the wisdom of the picnic I had suggested to Professor Palmer. In the air-conditioned lounge it had sounded just dandy, but, after walking a couple of blocks under a hot sun, I wondered if eating lunch in some dimly lit, cool restaurant wouldn't be better than a picnic amid the car sculptures of Carhenge.

Distracted with my load of thoughts and dazzled by the bright sun, I didn't see the lady emerging from the Laundromat with her own burden. Hers happened to be clean laundry.

She was nice enough about it, as I got down on my knees to help her retrieve the once carefully folded shirts and underwear. It was Mrs. Connaugh, owner of the Slick Whistle Laundromat where I did my washing when I was in town.

"And what are we up to this summer, Professor?" she asked sweetly. "Besides woolgathering, I mean."

Perceptive woman, I thought. "Another summer course," I said. "When I ran into you, I was thinking about Carhenge and Cass Deering."

"Aliens," she said.

"Aliens?" I asked.

"Or those ghost spirits. But I think it was aliens."

Mrs. Connaugh, I should explain, does more than operate the coin Laundromat. She also takes in overnight washing, which means she spends many a late evening among the machines listening to a national late-night talk show in which paranoids and late-night neurotics phone in to recount their abduction by flying saucers or to explain how crop circles are made by little green men emitting magnetic laser beams from their foreheads. In short, she's a Believer.

"Aliens," she repeated with a meaningful look. "That

poor girl. Just their type, too. Just whisked her away for their experiments, and dropped her somewhere when they were done with her. I bet she's wandering some big city without a clue who she is. When they experiment on you, they always give you amnesia afterward."

"Why do that?" I asked.

"So you won't remember, of course."

"But in Cass's case there was another person involved, the guy who was stabbed."

Mrs. Connaugh gave me the tut-tut look. If she hadn't been using both hands to hold her basket, she would have patted my arm with that indulgent patience people such as she use when talking to naïve children or the mentally challenged.

"Don't you know," she confided in a half whisper, looking around to be sure the aliens weren't eavesdropping, "with their minds they can control people to do things. I wouldn't be a bit surprised if they didn't make poor Cassie stab that man."

"I see," I said. Call me uncaring, but I didn't really want to go much further with this conversation. "What about the ghosts?"

"Carhenge," she confided to me, looking in the direction of that local monument to Detroit excessiveness.

"Ghosts?"

"Oh, aye! Dogs howling out there for no reason. People, going past it at night, see things, too . . . like gray phantoms among the cars. And there are those who have heard rattling and moaning noises, too!"

Maybe a restaurant was a better idea, after all. I looked at my watch.

"Oh, I need to go, Missus Connaugh, but it's nice to see you again. I'm really sorry I ran into you like I did. If any of those things need to be washed again, I'll gladly pay for it. I hope you're not hurt."

The washing was unsoiled, save for a few bits of sidewalk sand that brushed right off, and, as for my doing her any bodily harm by running into her, she assured me that it would take more than a mere lightweight such as myself to cause her damage. Silently I agreed. I'm not that light-weight, but if something were to make an impression on Mrs. Connaugh, it would have to be something bigger than me.

Back at the trailer, I dumped my classroom stuff on the table and got rid of the necktie. I got the plaid car robe off the bed and folded it, then dusted Horse's passenger side seat and drove to the SavaBuck Food Store to see what I could round up in the way of picnic viands. Eating in an air-conditioned restaurant would be more comfortable, but it would be more fun to watch Henriette Palmer in a tight skirt sitting on a car robe trying to get the plastic shrink-wrap off her dill pickle. Then, again, she'd probably insist on sitting at a picnic table. But table or no table, a picnic at Carhenge amounted to eating at an auto salvage yard.

Naturally the idea of taking a classy lady for a picnic among abandoned cars appealed to me.

Chapter Five

One pairing is as good as another
Where all is venture!
"The Contretemps"
—Thomas Hardy

Hank's Buick was parked in the shade of the elm next to my trailer as I drove up. She stepped out of the car, wearing khaki shorts, a sleeveless cotton shirt, sandals, and a floppy straw hat. She looked pretty enough to make me forget my skirt-on-the-blanket fantasy.

"A new outfit!" I observed. "Did you change clothes in the car?" Talk about fantasies.

"No. I told you I'd rent a room."

"And did you figure out which of these trailers was mine by looking at license plates," I said, "or did somebody tell you?" She nodded in the direction of the young man who was raking the tiny yard behind the trailer park office. Her informant. One look at those gams and the kid would have told her the combination to Fort Knox.

"Is that the picnic?" She smiled, looking at the cheap Styrofoam cooler I had just purchased along with the lunch supplies. I took it off the front seat and put it in the truck bed, securing it to the spare tire with a bungee cord.

"That's it," I said. "I bought it and a bag of ice to keep the champagne and caviar chilled."

"Champagne and caviar. Why don't I believe that?" she mused. "More like Coors and bologna, maybe?"

65

"We'll see," I said.

"We could take my car," Hank said wistfully as I opened Horse's door so she could climb into the cab.

"Thanks, but my local image could use a boost," I said, walking around to my own side. "When people see me with a classy gal in my truck, my credit will really go up."

"And I'm sure it will do wonders for mine," she muttered as she clanged the door shut. "When we get ready to leave Carhenge, I hope the cops don't think you're making off with one of the junk vehicles."

"Wrong color." I laughed, jamming Horse into gear. "Theirs are all gray."

In 1998, *Omaha World Herald* columnist Tony Moton uncorked the proverbial can of fish bait by asking how a certain travel writer could've explored Nebraska's automobile culture without mentioning Carhenge.

An anonymous reader replied—"The less said about that pile of junk the better."—while a more discerning critic called it "a classically eccentric piece of American folk art." Everyone, it seems, has an opinion about Alliance's big circle of recycled cars.

But the first time I went there, I took the advice of a Nebraska poet I know, a man who has been all over the British Isles and has seen dozens of stone circles, including Stonehenge, the model for Carhenge. "Park at the entrance," he said, "but don't go straight down the path toward the sculpture. Don't even look at it if you can help it. As soon as you walk through the fence, turn left and walk as far north as you can, then east. Go all the way to the top of the hill. Then bushwhack your way through the weeds back toward Carhenge from the northeast and you'll see something. And go early in the morning or at sunset."

I did as he suggested, and he was right. Viewed from the rise of ground to the northeast and in late evening, Carhenge is no longer a collection of car bodies. It is a monument to the vast and spreading plains beyond it, one of man's timeless and ancient ideas embodied in modern materials. Here are the great machines that conquered the infinite distances. Here stand solid steel cars and durable trucks imbedded in the implacable earth, saying: "We came this far, and here we remain." The looming rocks of Stonehenge planted in the Plain of Salisbury say much the same thing about their culture, and little more.

It is uncanny, the twilight view from the hill. The cars in the circle are half buried in the earth, some pointing skyward like ICBMs emerging from underground bunkers, others buried nose downward as if they had plunged from the sky straight into this Nebraska field.

Around the circle, other cars are up in the air, welded across the uprights like lintels and arches. There's an inner circle of monolithic car bodies, some of them angling into the ground like massive fallen lintel stones. An upside-down sedan represents another fallen lintel, and there is a car half buried outside the circle, out in the grass and weeds, right where the heel stone at Stonehenge's is placed.

The entire sculpture is painted dead stone gray, every car and station wagon and pickup truck. The glass has been removed from each vehicle and sheet metal is welded over the openings. The sheet metal is also a dead gray color.

Taking the poet's indirect route, I walked up a low rise of ground northeast of another sculpture, five car bodies welded into a tribute to Vivaldi. "The Fourd Seasons", it's called.

From the summit of the rise I looked back down toward Carhenge. An evening storm was building up out west, behind the circle of cars and behind the town. Moist air and updrafts were roiling up big heavy clouds the color of old pewter. They were being drawn out and hammered into long airborne ridges and queer valleys hanging inverted over the plains. Below the lowering sky, the dark green wheat field horizon was broken here and there by scatterings of trees and thickets. In the evening light it resembled Thomas Hardy's English countryside with its "piecework of harrowed fields and network of hedge."

Under the horizon line, squatting down defiantly beneath the approaching storm, Stonehenge appeared to me. Not Carhenge. Stonehenge. From that distance and in that light and with that particular backdrop, it looked mysterious and secret—silent steel pillars awaiting the coming of robed druids. The upright car bodies seemed to be leaning in toward one another, tightening the circle, as though to protect whatever secrets lingered within the enigmatic ring of hollow steel.

I wanted Professor Palmer to see it that way, too. She had been there a couple of times when she did her summer teaching at Alliance and found it mildly interesting, but I knew she hadn't seen it through the poet's eyes.

There's this about Hank: she's a helluva good sport. We left Horse in the little parking area and walked through the gate, then I turned to the left and led her through the weeds and sandburs, warning her not to look back at the assemblage of old cars. At the top of the hill by the "Fourd Seasons" sculpture I said—"Now."—and she turned and she, too, gave a gasp. Not so many clouds this time, just a scattering on the horizon. The sun was almost down, piercing the gray arches with long strips of dazzling light.

"Incredible," she said. "It's just incredible! If I squint my eyes a little, I can imagine I'm standing out on Salisbury

Plain, looking at Stonehenge. Have you ever seen a book titled *Stonehenge Complete*? By Christopher Chippindale?"

"Nope," I said, gazing away over the plains.

"Chippindale collected hundreds of old drawings and sketches of Stonehenge, some of them going back hundreds of years. Standing here makes me think of those old drawings, before they built the highways and the fences around Stonehenge. Almost eerie, isn't it?"

"Eerie," I said. "Why don't we eat?"

Since there were no guards or caretakers or even a sign prohibiting it, we took a chance and spread the car robe on the ground inside the fence, away from the picnic tables and parking lot. I had lied about the caviar. But at the SavaBuck Food Store I found three very credible varieties of gourmet cheese, some excellent water crackers, a light but spicy sausage, and, best of all, slender loaves of Bohemian rye bread from the local bakery. At the liquor depot next door I bought a bottle of Mumm's. It was an extra dry and not a brut, but it had looked classy enough to go with Professor Palmer's business suit. It was certainly appropriate with khaki shorts. Served in the plain glass flutes from the trailer—the cheese, bread, and sliced apples on china plates from the same source—this blanket picnic was nothing to apologize for.

Between bites and sips we watched the prairie sun slide down to touch the distant horizon and turn molten red. The skyline became a brilliant yellow and in a few minutes the thick storm clouds slid over the light as if someone had drawn the curtain. But the prairie storm was many miles away to the west; over us and all around us the sky remained clean and clear. What's the word for that particular transparent topaz color that the sky takes on just after sunset?

Unseen winds swept the curtaining clouds farther north-
ward until the remaining afterglow of the sun was once
more revealed. Streaks of evening light rushed across the
fields and hills. Carhenge took on deeply mysterious
shadows. In the background, distant buildings became low
black shapes cowering next to the shapeless dark silhouettes
of hulking ancient cottonwood groves.

"Hey!" I said, so suddenly that Hank fumbled her slice
of Bohemian bread, "speaking of facts and data, let me
show you something before it gets dark. Come on."

I led the way inside the circle of upright car bodies and
stopped next to two station wagons supporting a late '40s
Plymouth sedan as a lintel.

"I looked up the Stonehenge statistics on the college
computer last summer," I explained. "Count our paces."

Side by side, we walked around the inside of the circle
counting our steps. When we came back to the upright station wagons, I said: "Well?"

"Thirty-five or thirty-six," she said. "So what?"

"Do you know the inside diameter of Stonehenge?"

"No. But I do know it's smaller than you think it's going
to be, when you get there."

"Thirty-three meters. A hundred and eight feet. Now
multiply your thirty-six paces by three feet and you have the
same dimension. How many upright stones in Stonehenge?"

"I don't know. Twenty or thirty."

"Thirty," I said. "Count the cars, you get thirty. Those
stones at Stonehenge. . . ."

"The sarsens," she interrupted.

"The sarsens. They average four meters from ground to
top, which is thirteen feet. Two meters wide, which is six
and a half feet. And they're about one meter thick . . . three

feet. These Cadillac and Ford wagons are almost the same size. In other words, the guys who collected all these hulks and welded them together weren't just playing around with their tractors and front-end loaders. They built this thing to scale!"

"Interesting," Professor Palmer mused. And she meant it; she had that studious brow-furrowing look, the look of an academic considering a topic for a professional paper. Carhenge is more than a collection of junk cars. It's a full-scale model of England's best-known stone circle.

We fooled around at Carhenge a while longer—OK, so "fooled around" is a poor word choice—trying to see into some of the cars, trying to decipher the broken and painted-over metal lettering, trying to give each car a kind of story. The big Cadillac, the Ford station wagon, the Jeep pickup, the elderly Plymouth, each had its own history if it could talk. Somebody, somewhere had earned money to buy that car, had taken pride in it. It had driven people to work, to the store, to the bank, to the hospital, to the graveyard to bury some loved one. But then it was traded in, given away, sold, or wrecked, over and over, until it ended up here, window openings sealed with sheet metal, factory finish painted dull gray, welded to another car until rust do them part.

It reminded me of the protagonists inhabiting last summer's novels, the women for whom the books were named. Born, nurtured, cared for, and neglected, never fully understood by anyone, handed off and handed around and finally abandoned. Such has been the fate of uncountable women, real as well as fictional. Some few of them, like these silent remnants of automobiles, live on as a kind of art, cold, mute monuments to the dignity and style that remains when the labor of living has passed away.

★ ★ ★ ★ ★

We packed up and I drove Hank back to the trailer park to retrieve her Buick, but neither of us felt like calling it a night. Those long summer evenings are hard to let go of. The sun was down, but the prairie world was still light. And it was cooler. Time to stroll the streets and look into the windows of closed shops. Time to drive down to the river with a fishin' pole and six-pack. Time to go to the movies or to the Dairy Queen for a swirl cone.

On the drive back I had told Hank about Cass Deering and her sister, but not about what her sister did for a living. So now I said: "I've got an idea. Are you up to a forty mile drive this evening?" It was more like fifty, but I was planning to take her Buick and didn't want to make her hesitant.

"What for?" she said. I would have corrected her diction, but her car is so much more comfortable than Horse.

"To see Cass Deering's sister," I said. "Over in Morris."

"Do you know where to find her? She won't mind us showing up unexpectedly, will she? You might phone her and warn her we're coming."

"Uh, no. She won't mind. She works over there. Probably working tonight, so we'd be more like customers."

Professor Henriette Palmer studied my face the way she would study one of her historical documents for flaws and hidden meanings.

"What are you up to?"

"Nothing. I just thought we might talk to her and find out something. Something the cops didn't think about. That's all. Cross my heart."

"I want to stop at the motel and change out of these shorts," Hank said.

"Fine. I'll come with you. It's on the way."

72

"Aha!" she said, poking a finger firmly into my chest. "That's it! You just want to engage in a little personal sight-seeing, you lech."

A rhetorical dilemma. I couldn't very well say I *didn't* want to watch, while at the same time I couldn't tell her we were going to visit a strip joint. Which wasn't my main motive, either. Honest.

"Hey, I'll wait in the car, of course! I'm not the kind of guy to ply a woman with champagne and then help her out of her shorts."

"Hah! And who said we're taking my car?"

"Would you rather ride all that way in my truck?"

"We'll take the car. And *you* will fasten your seatbelt and leave it fastened until we get to Morris."

"Nuts."

So once again I found myself on the wide two-lane with the radio playing, the air conditioning on low, and the wheat fields and the cornfields whizzing past. The corner of my eye registered the staccato punctuation of telephone poles—*whup, whup, whup, whup*—and the four-strand barbed-wire fences stretched between posts like musical staves on which the notes have yet to be written. Here a diesel tractor pumped black exhaust heavenward as it carried the farmer home from his long day in the fields. There a hawk hunted the twilight stubble between giant rolls of last year's hay. Every living creature seemed to be playing its part in one of the thousand life-and-death dramas of evening on the prairie.

Farmhouses and farm barns and farm fences always look cleaner and neater in the twilight. They seem at peace after the day's work. Only with great difficulty could one imagine any conflict behind those walls, any anger within those fences and windbreaks. Yet a man could lie stabbed with a butcher knife in a remote farmhouse just as easily as he could lie in his own blood in an apartment over a garage in town. Behind those walls and curtains were women just like the ones in the novels, a whole population of Carries and Janes and Ántonias and Maggies and, yes, even Lolitas, washing the supper dishes or watching the television while imagining themselves outside the walls, beyond the fences, somewhere, anywhere else.

Cass Deering knew it. She lived among them all her life, these prairie people who, despite their urban ways, are still symbols and embodiments of mortality's endless patterns. If they could read their own stories as writers see them, Cass must have thought, if they could read how each act and each decision would play out into a series of predictable consequences, perhaps they could change the outcome. Or accept it with self-awareness, at least.

"What are you thinking about?" Hank asked without taking her eyes from the road.

I turned from the window and looked, instead, at the line of white dashes on the asphalt like Morse code rushing under the car. "Oh, everything and nothing, I guess. The turn-off's just ahead."

I hadn't been in Morris before and didn't know where the strip club was, but I knew where it would probably be. Every small Western town seems to be laid out the same way—two or three blocks of businesses, surrounded on two or three sides by a series of residential streets. Look for elm trees if you want to find the residential neighborhoods. Across town there's usually a grain elevator and a railroad station; go in that direction if you're looking for the co-op store or the lumberyard or the guy who does welding and radiator repair. Beyond the tracks, you find the boarded-up dance hall, bowling alley, or roller skating arena, several vacant lots full of weeds, a new liquor store or beer joint managing to hang on by its toenails, and, if there is one, the club.

I pointed to the garish neon sign that said **THE BOOTSTRAP CLUB** and to the parking lot just off the street.

Professor Palmer put on the brakes in the middle of the street and turned on me. Turned to me. Well, both.

"*Here?*" she said, eyeing the sign's undulating graphics. "Here? A strip joint?"

"It's a gentlemen's club," I explained in my best and most formal academic tone. "A place where hard-working guys unwind after a long day's work. Cass's sister is a dancer here. See what the sign says? Twenty beautiful dancers. OK, so it probably means twenty beautiful dancers since the place was built. Still, I'll bet there are three or four per night."

"And you expect me to go in there with you?" she asked incredulously.

"You could wait in the car," I said.

"I *could* leave you out here on the sidewalk!" she said. "You *could* suddenly find yourself strolling back to your little tin trailer in Alliance."

We pulled off the street and continued our discussion, one reasonable academic to another, and in the end it was Professor Henriette Palmer's inborn sense of adventure and fun that did the trick. She was curious. She didn't admit it. I admitted it for her, which is just as good.

We went in "to get it over with, as long as we're here," as she said, and Hank's mood lightened up when the door gorilla tapped me for the ten-dollar cover charge. Twenty bucks and I hadn't seen anything except Hank Palmer in loose slacks and a light jacket—and the primate bouncer, who I would have paid twenty bucks *not* to see.

Inside, we found an empty table, a small one back in the shadows. The other patrons of the ecdysiast's art, maybe two dozen of them, were seated right up around a raised platform, pushing their beer mugs around on a narrow ledge while they waited for the next dancer to appear. I saw a white shirt and necktie standing in the shadows with a human figure crammed into it and beckoned him over.

"Yeah?" he inquired.

"Good evening." I smiled. "I wonder . . . does a dancer named Deering work here?"

"Nah. And we don't give out no names."

"I see," I said. End of conversation. A sort of waitress teetered up to our table, her high spike heels and low-cut cleavage creating a symphony of anatomical movement best described as a temptation of gravity, that, or an ultimate test of the tensile strength in man-made fabric. Hank and I each ordered a beer. $5 a glass, draught. The fancy stuff—which meant anything in a longneck bottle—started at $6.50, and I didn't even ask how much they would charge for Scotch.

"Can't I have champagne?" Hank asked with evil intent.

"Not at these prices, you don't. You wouldn't even get beer, except that we have to either order something or get tossed out of here. If we have a drink, we're customers. If not, we're just voyeurs who want to look at naked women."

"*I'm* a voyeur of women?" she said indignantly.

I raised an eyebrow and tilted my head an inch to indicate it might be a possibility. Or the management might see it that way.

"Wonderful," she muttered. "Just wonderful."

The stage floodlight came on and the revolving ball of

mirrors began to throw little squares of light around on the ceiling and walls. The first dancer went into her act.

Two dancers later, I was on my second beer and Professor P. was casting anxious looks toward the little girl's room. To get to it, she was going to have to walk past the all-male audience, one of the largest collections of blue collars outside of the JCPenney catalog.

The third dancer appeared, head tilted back, face lifted upward at the mirrored ball, long legs arched, arms crossed seductively over the see-through costume she would soon discard. Her music throbbed through the dark joint, chasing the little squares of light. She wheeled on one toe, lightly took hold of the fireman's pole center stage, went into a deep split, rose again on the pole with her back to it, polishing the brass with what little remained of her costume. I watched carefully, wishing I had my notebook. This was my kind of research. I felt like Mark Twain sitting down on the clothes of some Hawaiian girls he discovered bathing, feeling it was his obligation to report on this kind of local color for his newspaper.

"That's her," I said.

"How do you know?" Hank asked.

"Because she looks just like Cass Deering. Younger, I'd guess. But the same face."

"And how do we get to talk with her?" Hank asked. "I get the impression that customers are discouraged from fraternizing with the performers."

"I get the impression they'd break your arms just for asking."

"Excuse me," Hank said, rising. Too much excitement, or too much beer, or both.

While she was in the back of the building, no doubt studying the classic features of American midland restroom architecture, I managed to catch the eye of another white shirt and tie; this one appeared able to score a little higher on a high school verbal test.

"Help you?" he said, continuing to watch Cass's sister rather than look at me.

"Know Bob Houghton, over in Alliance?"

"Yeah."

"I'm helping him keep the Cass Deering case open. Not officially. County won't finance any more official investigations."

"How do I know that?" he asked suspiciously.

"You could call Houghton. Phone him at home, if you want to," I said.

"And you want to talk to her sister."

"Right."

He mulled it over. In fact, between mulling and watching the girl dance, he seemed to lose track of the issue altogether. But Hank came back at that moment and smiled sweetly at him as she resumed her seat.

"You with him?" the man said.

"Yes," she said. She no doubt wanted to say something cute, but, with twenty or thirty native boys out there ready to walk her to the parking lot, she preferred to admit she was, indeed, *with* me.

"You can talk to her," he said, pointing at Palmer. "She'll be off in a coupla minutes. I'll come get you."

The interval provided Professor Palmer with adequate time to explain her opinions (plural) of any slime ball that would bring a lady to such a place, and then let a man who looked like King Kong's sparring partner drag her off to the back room, and just because the aforementioned slime ball wanted access to a stripper. She explained it all rather succinctly, I thought. But Hank is nothing if not a sport, so, when the manager came to get her, she swiveled up off her chair and followed him, but not without giving me what novelists call a "departing glance". In her case a "departing glance" involves clenched teeth and a fiery glare in the eyes.

Palmer was gone long enough for me to have another $5 beer and pay a visit to the boys' room. The bits of wit and philosophy written on the walls were professionally comforting; apparently there is still a crying need for English teachers in this world. Talk about poor diction. And worse grammar. The clichés were appalling, too.

My "research assistant" returned after a half hour, and just in time. The first dancer had started the second set of the evening and the house ape was giving me a buy-another-beer-or-get-out look. So I took Professor Palmer and got out.

Once we had the Buick headed back up the highway, windows wide open to air the cigarette stench out of our clothes, she handed me a slip of paper.

"Her phone number and address," she said. "She usually gets up around one in the afternoon and wouldn't mind talking to you. She seems glad to hear that someone is still interested in her sister's disappearance."

"I owe you one," I said.

Hank was in a meditative sort of mood as she drove.

"You know," she said, "she seems like a really nice young lady. She reads. She saves her money. She plans to save enough to go to college or start a business of her own. And did you know, those girls make more money in one night. . . ."

". . . than professors do in a month?" I volunteered.

"In a week, anyway. I had no idea they earned so much. Much of it is in tips, but, still, it's a lot of money. And the club takes good care of them. They have security men who walk them to their cars after closing time. If they've seen any customers who look suspicious, the security men follow the girls home and hang around to make sure they're safe. She has to stay in shape, too. I have a little more respect for club dancers after talking to her."

At this point you're probably thinking I'll make some lewd remark about Professor Palmer's potential as a dancer and ask her why she doesn't give up teaching and go into stripping. But a highway at midnight at least twenty miles from town seemed like a poor place to be pushed out of a moving car.

Chapter Six

The compensation of growing old, Peter Walsh
thought, was simply this: that the passions remained
as strong as ever, but one has gained—at last!—the
power which adds the supreme flavour to exis-
tence,—the power of taking hold of experience, of
turning it round, slowly, in the light.

Mrs. Dalloway
—Virginia Woolf

The figure seated on the bench in the hallway was Margaret
Street, and she was waiting for me. She rose at my approach, a trim and mature woman whose only flaw was an
apparent obsession with the color pink.

"Professor McIntyre." She said it as if announcing me to
someone.

"Good morning, Missus Street. Something I can do for
you?"

"I was wondering if we might talk."

"Certainly," I said. "After class?"

"Perhaps this afternoon?" she countered. "Say, around
three o'clock? I need to do some shopping and I was
thinking we might meet at the Bistro. They do a lovely raspberry trifle and tea."

Raspberry trifle and tea. I knew the place she meant;
right in the middle of this farm town, it's a tastefully decorated upscale place for people who like ambiance with their
gourmet coffee. Well, I thought, some good Earl Grey and a

blueberry muffin on a china plate would be a nice change from drinking cold Budweisers in the Homesteader.

Class was OK that day, but nothing to write home about. Word had got out, as word does, that I had been mentioning Cass Deering's name around town, with the result that the students were more interested in discussing her than in hearing the nuances of Wordsworth's definition of common.

"Common sense, to Wordsworth, simply meant anything that everyone senses in common. That is, we all agree that we see it, or we all agree that it makes sense. In poetry, he and others . . . like Coleridge . . . strove to find themes that appealed to commonly held beliefs, experiences held in common. Mister Martley, do you have an example for us?"

"I guess 'Strange Fits of Passion Have I Known' would be an example. Everybody's had that feeling, sometime or other. But. . . ."

"Yes?"

"Do you think Cass Deering was also murdered? Maybe by the same person who murdered Deerfield?"

So it went, and the three hours seemed longer than usual. Eventually it limped and dragged itself to a weary close, and after two brief student conferences I managed to get away to grab a sandwich.

Mid-afternoon found me attired in a reasonably crisp white shirt and conservative dark tie and seated across a table from Margaret Street at one of the Bistro's tables, deliberately chosen for its location in a corner well away from eavesdroppers. She had been shopping for a party, she told me, picking up candy and nuts for the little snack dishes and flowers for the entry hall and sideboard.

"Doctor Street loves to have the house look pretty for his parties," she explained, reaching over to touch the pile of bouquets she had placed on the adjoining table, "especially when we're entertaining some of the other college administrators and staff."

"I know the situation," I said. "My wife Aggie is also an administrator, you know. Several parties per semester. The kind requiring a general house cleaning and decorating."

We ordered our tea and moved the conversation along.

"First," she said, "I do want to apologize for dropping your class last summer. You see . . . in the first place . . . I don't have to pay tuition. Relatives of faculty and administrators may take a certain number of credits for free. I always try to take classes whenever I can, mostly out of a sense of obligation. Doctor Street thinks I should. But to be truthful, I don't really like to read all that much."

"I see," I said.

"Oh, but that's not the reason! Oh, no. No, the reason is the parties. Dick . . . my husband . . . simply won't hear of having anyone but me plan his parties. He's terribly active in the community. We seem to be on the go all the time. Last summer he was part of a group of community leaders . . . he's on the board of the Chamber of Commerce, you know . . . leaders from this part of the state . . . were invited to a four-day retreat at Fort Robinson. Have you been there? And right after *that*, his alumni group had a reunion. I had to help plan a luncheon and cocktail party and dinner for thirty people. That was when I had to drop the class. I was 'way behind on the reading assignments."

"You know, Missus Street, I'm glad you told me this. Frankly I'm afraid I tend to take it personally whenever any student drops my class. I usually wonder what I did to drive them away."

We made more small talk about the complexities of college administration.

Margaret ordered a second pot of tea, turned down a second helping of trifle, and came to her next point.

"I'm concerned about Cass Deering," she said confidentially.

"Oh," I said.

"There is a rumor she's working at a . . . well, a kind of club, over in Morris. But I'm afraid for her, very afraid."

"I heard the same thing," I said. "I went to see the young lady, though, and it's not Cass Deering. It's her sister."

"Oh, dear!"

"Yes. Nobody seems to know where Cass is, or even what happened that night."

"Oh, dear," she repeated. "Oh, dear."

There was a moment of stunned silence while she assimilated this situational shift and rearranged her mental furniture around it. Then Margaret leaned toward me and became even more confidential.

"It's this book," she said. She took her purse from a chair, the same chair that held her shopping bags of candy and flowers. From the purse she withdrew a slim gray volume with blue lettering. On the cover was a post-modern portrait of a shadowy figure wearing a cloche and carrying flowers. I looked at the title, although I already knew what it was. It was *Mrs. Dalloway*. By Virginia Woolf.

"You, too?" I said.

"Pardon?"

"I've been hearing that Cass gave novels to other friends of hers."

"Oh. I think she meant *this* one as more than just a gift between friends."

"Oh?"

"Now, Doctor McIntyre, I need you to promise me that

what I'm about to say will go no further. I don't know you well, but I do know people. I feel I can trust you. I wouldn't tell you this, but certain people have mentioned to me that you are looking into poor Cass's situation. That, and you do have a certain reputation for investigations."

"*Literary* investigations," I hastened to correct her. "I'm no detective."

"Anyway." She drew a deep breath, and it was clear she would not exhale again until she had rid her conscience of this awfully personal information she had. Her eyes scanned the other patrons to be certain they weren't listening. She swallowed hard several times and twisted her napkin with both hands before looking up into my face.

"Cass kissed me," she whispered.

OK . . . try sitting in a proper little tea shop in a small town with a stranger and have her confide in you that a younger woman kissed her, and see if you can come up with the next line of conversation. I certainly couldn't. So I just sat examining the surface of my tea and how it reflected the slowly turning overhead fan while I waited to find out why. Not why Cass Deering kissed her, but why I wanted to hear about it.

"I'll never forget it. So . . . so spontaneous. We ran into one another at the Fourth of July fireworks picnic . . . you know the sort of thing . . . and, as we talked, we rather naturally strolled away from the noisy crowd.

"We found ourselves in among the bushes on the other side of the pond . . . still on the path, you know, but out of sight of everyone . . . and we were laughing at each other's stories about skinny-dipping when we were children. I was saying how shocked the men would be to overhear us when she suddenly and simply kissed me. On the mouth."

"Well," was the most brilliant thing I could think of to say. "But what . . . ?"

"What does it have to do with anything?" she asked. "It's just that, later, she gave me this book . . . you've read it closely, I know . . . and she had marked it up! Look!"

Margaret Street pushed the novel across the table to me. I opened it at random, flipped through pages until I came to some underlining and handwriting in the margins. I read Woolfe's description of how Clarissa Dalloway can remember "scene after scene" of moments she spent with Peter, the energetic young man she liked—or loved—but did not marry. Cass had written in the margin—**It's like this, isn't it?**—and at the bottom of the page had written: **O, Margaret, we must not let these loves go, and then marry the wrong person.** On another page, Paul visits Clarissa Dalloway. She is irritated that she is still mending dresses and planning parties for her dull husband while Paul has traveled clear to India. **We CAN go to India, Margaret**, the handwritten note said.

Page after page, the novel was underlined and contained notes Cass made to draw scenes to Margaret Street's attention. But if I had been thinking the notes and underlinings were somehow aimed at some kind of seduction, I soon changed my mind. I did not know much about Margaret Street, yet I could see what Cass was probably trying to say to her friend.

"I don't quite understand," I lied, hoping Margaret would put my thoughts into words and save me the embarrassment. However, as I just said, I didn't know her well enough.

"At first, I thought she meant that she and I should run away and be lovers. Can you imagine my feelings about that? But that doesn't relate to anything in this book . . .

you see that, I'm sure . . . so I thought and thought and *thought* about it, and then I saw it. I saw what she meant. She was trying to tell me what she was going to do, you see. Oh! If only it hadn't taken me this long to see it!" Margaret paused and tears began to moisten the corners of her eyes.

"What she was going to do?" I echoed. "What *was* she going to do?"

"Murder that one man and run off with the other one, of course. Don't you see? Peter Walsh . . . the man in the novel . . . is Cass's first love. And Richard Deering . . . the man who was killed . . . he was like Clarissa Dalloway's dull husband. Cass didn't want to end up like Clarissa Dalloway. She wanted to get away from the man she couldn't stand and go away with the other one. It's the same in the novel. That's what I realized. Clarissa is just like Cass . . . they have the same curse. They understand everyone around them . . . everyone, just everyone! . . . and yet they have to go on living in a world of unending meaninglessness. Playing about and going to parties . . . that's what Peter says Clarissa is all about."

At this point she took the book from me as if she had just thought of something else. "Look, I'll show you something," she said.

For several minutes she flipped from page to page, back and forth, scanning passages Cass had underlined. Finally she returned it to me with her finger marking a spot. In the margin Cass had written—**No, no, no, no!**—just like that, over and over.

It was the passage in which Septimus, a character who was driven insane by seeing his friend killed in battle, is himself being driven further and further into a dark neurotic hell. Septimus talks about suicide throughout the novel and finally leaps from the upper window to impale himself on iron fence railings.

"You think. . . ."

"I think Cass was torn between two men, and she must have considered doing away with herself. I didn't think of that until just now! So those underlines and that 'no, no, no' isn't meant for me after all . . . you see what I mean? . . . she thought she saw the way out. *She* thought of suicide. Oh, Doctor McIntyre, I'm afraid she's done it. I wonder if she's drowned herself. In the novel, Clarissa Dalloway thinks about the deep sea and the waves, you know. She thinks about the peacefulness. Cass often told me how much she loved peacefulness as a little girl."

"Somebody else mentioned drowning to me," I said. "Well, I'll certainly think about all this," I said as I rose and began making gotta-go noises.

"C.D."

"Pardon?"

"Cass Deering. Clarissa Dalloway. C.D. They have the same initials."

A friend of Margaret's came in at that point and made a beeline for our table, so I said good bye again, and left.

Outside, the summer sun was bleaching the sidewalk and the heat was rising in waves from the parked cars, but I didn't seem to notice it as much as usual. My mind was too busy churning the possibilities raised by Margaret.

She was definitely wrong about one thing: Clarissa Dalloway was not Cass Deering. It was Margaret Street who had the dull husband, whose life seemed centered on parties and conservative newspapers, the only two sources of his own views and opinions. It was Margaret who was out shopping for flowers. God, didn't she recognize herself in the very opening of the novel? "Mrs. Dalloway said she would buy the flowers herself." Perhaps—my imagination was racing—perhaps the reason for that spontaneous kiss on the lips was Cass Deering's recognizing a hidden sensuality in Margaret, a passion concealed and presumably lost. Cass read the novel, saw Margaret in it, and surmised there might have been a young and energetic love in her earlier life. She guessed that Margaret had married Francis Street for what . . . security? Status? Because he asked her to and she could think of no reason *not* to?

Go find your Peter Walsh. *That's* what Cass was trying to tell Margaret by giving her a copy of Woolf's novel. Look at Mrs. Dalloway and do something or you'll end up just like her.

Whatever had gone through Cass's mind as she had marked and annotated the novel, it was not that she saw herself as Clarissa Dalloway. The initials C.D. didn't stand for Cass Deerfield.

They stood for Margaret Street.

Chapter Seven

Though often disillusioned, she was still waiting for
that halcyon day when she should be led forth
among dreams become real. . . . It was forever to be
the pursuit of that radiance of delight which tints the
distant hilltops of the world. Oh, Carrie! . . . You
dream such happiness as you may never feel.

Sister Carrie
—Theodore Dreiser

Saturday morning I awoke early and restless. As I dressed, I considered taking Pat Kisimoto up on his invitation to practice with the local *bojutsu* group. Pat was one of the building custodians at the Learning Center; during my first week on campus, last summer, I saw him carrying a *bojutsu* stick and discovered we had a mutual interest in stick fighting. When he heard I had come back for a second summer, Pat wasted no time looking me up.

"Doc!" he had said, catching me heading for class one day. "Saturday morning at the rec center! C'mon and work out with us."

But for some reason when Saturday rolled around, I didn't feel like it, even though it was probably just what I needed. When you're nervous and restless and don't know why, getting your noggin bopped and your belly jabbed can be a helpful way to start the day. This morning, though, I seemed to need something else.

I walked over to Houghton's Hut, hoping coffee and

breakfast would help. After breakfast, along toward noon, I'd call Cass's sister and arrange to meet her in Morris. That's what was making me edgy, I decided. Not the idea of talking to an exotic dancer, but the fact that I wanted to. It meant I was already drawn into this disappearance, and, worse yet, I started to see patterns everywhere I looked. My chat with Margaret Street bothered me more than I wanted to admit, mostly because of what it led me to infer about Cass Deering. I became more and more convinced she was the type who watches a TV show or a film or reads a book and puts herself in it, who sees her own hopes and fears and passions and frustrations being played out.

That sensation of walking out of a movie feeling like one of the characters you've been watching is temporary. It has usually worn off by the time you get home. But fiction is different. Fiction has always been recognized as having a powerful and pervasive effect on the human psyche. Ever since people learned to read, governments and churches have periodically burned or banned books out of fear that they would turn the minds of the populace. To mention a very minor example, I remember students being drawn to Edward Abbey's anarchists after reading *The Monkey Wrench Gang*, and others whose lives were changed by Alex Haley's *Roots*. Some of us old-timers still see the government as Big Brother, thanks to George Orwell, and 1984 was a long time ago.

Cass Deering seemed to see people she knew in every book she read. But the key question is what book did she see herself in? And if she *did* discover herself in a fictional character, how far did she go in following that character's fate? The more I thought about it, the more convinced I was that "we" (meaning myself) would find Cass Deering's trail as soon as we found that book.

The Hut was busy when I got there, but Ed, the Home-steader bartender, waved to me and pointed to the empty seat across from him. Ed looked like he could use a nap, and it was still early morning. Bob Houghton was in his jeans and sport shirt behind the counter, refilling the coffee urn, and he, too, looked like a man who had been danced on all night. When he finished with the urn, he came to the table with two plates of the trucker's friend, a big breakfast of pancakes, eggs, sausages, and home fries. He put one in front of Ed and sat down to the other himself.

"How y'doin', Doc?" Bob asked.

"Good," I said. "Better than you two, I'd say. You look like you've been up all night."

"Good guess," Ed said. He was wearing a blue uniform shirt with a badge pinned to it. The badge said **Animal Control Officer**.

"What happened?" I asked.

Edna poured me a cup of coffee and took my order.

"Same thing that happens every couple of weeks about this time of year," the sergeant said. "Kids go out to Carhenge to neck and drink and they start hearing weird noises. Or think they see wild dogs. Sometimes the neighbors hear howling and shouting, if the wind is in their direction. So, somebody calls me and I call our friendly local neighborhood dog-catcher and get him out of bed . . . right, Ed? . . . and we go out to Carhenge and spend all night trying to find wild dogs, stray dogs, whatever."

"Get any?"

"Never do. But we park out there a while, with the red light turning, and shine our flashlights around a lot, and people figure everything's under control. Sometimes . . . like last night . . . we fire a couple of shots into a dirt bank to make it sound like we're shooting at marauding packs of wild dogs."

"You're kidding, right? About the dog packs, I mean."

"Just kidding," Ed said as he ate. "They're actually only werewolves, but we don't advertise the fact. Drink your coffee."

The coffee was good and strong.

"A local lady told me aliens land at Carhenge and abduct women."

"That'd be Missus Connaugh." Sergeant Houghton laughed. "Ed, here, he told her once that we carry silver bullets in case we see werewolves out there. Or was it vampires?"

"So, why this time of year?" I persisted.

"Huh?" Ed said.

"You said it happens at this time of year."

"Oh," Ed said. "In the summer, more people go out to Carhenge for picnics. Some of the window panels in the cars are bent or missing, so they use 'em for trash cans for their sandwich wrappers and potato chip bags. Then the rats and gophers get into the cars after the garbage and dogs get after the rodents. Sometimes coyotes come around. We see their tracks and the droppings, but never do find the animals."

Bob stopped putting home fries into his face long enough to add his two cents' worth. "In the summer, the kids like to park out there . . . well, they aren't *all* kids. Some of the town's higher-class extramarital affairs start out there. Anyway, they're out there with the windows rolled down because it's summer. Or they take a blanket and go hide behind some of the cars, and the next thing you know they think they hear werewolves or aliens prowling the place. It's pretty spooky, on a dark night."

"Don't forget Ronnie Webber," Ed said.

"Oh, yeah . . . Ronnie. Once in a while the noises and strange lights turn out to be Ronnie, trying to get something off one of the cars, a muffler or a drive shaft or something. I've warned him three or four times."

Edna brought me my Denver omelet and the conversation turned to such other concerns as the weather, the local sports, the condition of Highway 2, and what-the-hell-was-going-on-with-gas-prices. Bob Houghton asked Edna, and then his wife Betty herself to bring him another plate load of home fries from the café kitchen he was half owner of. And he was turned down.

"We reserve the right," Betty said, pointing to the sign over the register, "to refuse second helpings to anyone."

"So," he said, folding his napkin beside his coffee cup and changing the subject, "you going over to Morris to talk to Debbie?"

"How did you know about that?"

"Word gets around."

"No kidding! You don't mind if I snoop around and ask questions about this murder and disappearance thing?"

"I don't care. If anybody files a complaint that you're harassing them, I'll lock you up, but, otherwise, she's still a free country. God knows I don't have the resources to keep on investigating a year-old missing person case. The state police have her on their wanted list, so sooner or later she'll turn up. Our own budget is too small. We even have to depend on volunteers like Ed here."

"Volunteer," Ed snorted. "Volunteer means you pay for your own breakfast."

I gassed up Horse, phoned home to learn that Aggie was playing hooky from her administration responsibilities to visit her sister in Michigan, then phoned the number Hank had written down for me. I caught Debbie Deering just as she was leaving her house to take a load of wash to the Laundromat. She said she'd meet me at the Dairy Queen in a couple of hours.

Just for the heck of it, I drove to Morris along the asphalt and gravel section roads, those thin black lines on the map that divide the Great Plains into squares. It's good to cruise along with the windows open so you won't miss the bright glint of irrigation water pouring over a measuring flume, or the sight of a Dempster or Aeromotor turning slowly in the breeze, the pump rod rising and falling in lazy rhythm. You're more apt to smile at the sight of two horses running across a pasture, manes tossing from arched necks and tails flying like silken banners. Going past one farm, I slowed down and then stopped to watch a tractor plowing. It was almost at the end of the furrow, and I just wanted to see the tumblebug plow flip over as it turned to go back up the field.

From time to time I saw nonmoving things, long ignored by human beings, like an abandoned farmhouse or an old car body rusting away in a gully. I saw a windmill with its wheel all bent and hanging like a bird with a broken neck. I saw a moldering haystack that hard-working hands had built so the livestock would have winter feed, now black and rotting back into the dark earth. Even in these disused human things, however, were reminders of the life and energy that had gone into them.

I wouldn't have recognized Debbie Deering except she was the only woman sitting outside the Dairy Queen with a basket of freshly folded laundry. At the strip club she had a flying cascade of shoulder-length blonde hair, a tanned body glistening with oil and metallic glitter, heavy mascara and lipstick, exaggerated eyelashes, tall spike heels. The girl sitting at the metal table quietly inhaling her cigarette had her hair tucked up under a baseball cap, wore little lipstick and no eye shadow, and was dressed in faded jeans and a sloppy T-shirt. She didn't even look as tall as she had on stage.

We got on easily and quickly. I asked if she had been waiting long, and she said no, that it had given her a chance to fold her laundry and enjoy the sunshine. She ordered a Coke and a basket of chicken strips, and I ordered a sooper-size malted milk that turned out to have the consistency of wall spackle. We talked about the weather, the towns, books, and my job. We talked about teaching, mainly how neither of us would want to go into secondary school teaching. We talked about places we both had been—Denver, Omaha, Minneapolis—and very gradually and very naturally the topic of her sister came up.

"I think Sergeant Houghton is right," she admitted. "I think Cass did kill Carl. What a scum ball! I can even imagine what happened. I'll bet he came home and started to pick a fight. He had a snooty way about him. He looked down his nose at everyone, and he had a way of sniffing through his nose at you when you said something. It made you feel like he knew everything, was always right about everything, and you were dumb as dirt."

"What do you think she saw in him?" I asked gently.

"God knows. But he pretty much ran her life after he came back. I don't know where he'd been . . . she never told me, so I didn't even know he'd more or less abandoned her . . . but he came back. After that, he made her wear weird clothes, wouldn't let her go out and get a job. She couldn't go anywhere in the evenings at all. And you know what? He was possessive and jealous and manipulating and all that, but I think he was sleeping around on her. I don't know, but I'm pretty sure. He even came on to me once, but I told him where to go."

"But for her to kill him with a butcher knife . . . ," I suggested.

"You didn't know him. Most people just walked away from him when he started to argue. If you didn't, you'd want to hit him. You'd talk to him for a few minutes, about anything, and he'd turn it into a yelling match. And he was one of those people you can't ever find an answer for. I mean, they say something really aggravating and you're stumped at what to say back to them, so you get all frustrated and walk away. And cooped up in that little room, nowhere to go, maybe Cass was using the knife to fix supper and he started in on her. She could have wanted him to shut up for a while. Or maybe she went to the kitchen to get away from him, and he followed her, and then she picked up the knife and told him to get out. I can see her doing that."

We were quiet for a few minutes. Debbie finished her chicken strips, and I dug at the thick malted milk with my straw. Finally she spoke again.

"Maybe Cass told Carl she was through with him and was going back with Michael. That could've made him mad enough to hit her."

"Now, this Michael . . . somebody else mentioned him. He was a former boyfriend?"

"Cass always told me he was the one. They were really in love, I think. But he had money issues, you know? Wanted to find a way to make a lot of money before getting married."

"Does Bob Houghton know about Michael?"

"Oh, sure. He even knew about it before he came to talk to me last summer. When he and I talked about it, we started to figure out that Cass and Michael were secretly married, maybe before he took off for South America, or wherever he went."

Debbie leaned forward and lowered her voice as if someone might be listening in on our conversation. "Personally, I think he's dead, too."

"Dead," I repeated. I was still trying to straighten out in my mind who this Michael was and now he's dead.

"I was over at the folks' house . . . Cass and I inherited it together . . . I guess we ought to sell it, but the money from the rent pays the taxes and the renters keep it up pretty good, so. . . ."

"What about Michael?"

"Oh. It was the last time I saw him. Or Cass, either. He didn't know the folks were dead and thought they'd know where she was. When he came looking, I just happened to be there. God, he looked awful! I hardly knew who he was! From what I gather, he was down in South America or Costa Rica or somewhere. Maybe Colombia. Trying to get rich quick. What's the name of that play where . . . ?"

Too sudden a turn for me. "What play?"

"Where that guy goes to Africa or Alaska or somewhere and comes back with diamonds. You know . . . his brother is stuck selling stockings or something?"

"*Death of a Salesman?*"

"That's it. Michael, he went somewhere weird like that. But he came back so sick! God! Something turned him all yellow like. He lost fifty pounds, I bet, and his hair got thin and all bleached out. He had big veins on his arms, too, all swollen. Horrible."

"He came back to take Cass away, you think?"

"I think so. Sergeant Houghton said he vanished from that motel in Alliance the same night she did. I don't think he killed Carl, though. He didn't look strong enough to cut his own meat, let alone stab a big healthy man to death. Maybe they went back to South America."

"They wouldn't just go to his family, wherever they live?" I asked.

"All he had was a father, somewhere in Colorado. I don't think his father had any money, but Michael must have got money from somebody, so he could go get rich in South America."

"And then he was coming back so they could get married?" I said.

"That's what she said. But we needed money right then, right away. It was always, always the problem. Dad had only a few months left, and the medical bills were unbelievable. Mom needed attention, too, and Cass and I together could just barely keep the monthly payments going. Then Cass got an idea that Carl would help us, and she went away to work for him. I don't know where. She never wrote or anything. God! She took it all on herself."

"I heard she was like that," I said.

"She was. Then something happened to whatever deal she had going with Carl when she got pregnant."

"Was it Michael who got her pregnant, you suppose?"

"Unfortunately I think it was Carl. I really do. I think she went to Scottsbluff, or wherever he was, met him, and got pregnant, then he didn't want anything to do with her. She wrote to Michael in care of his father, but he'd already. . . ."

"Gone to South America," I said.

"I guess. She got a job for a while over in Pershing at that electronics factory, but Dad died, and then Mom got sicker, and the baby was born too soon and died. She was at her wit's end, I think. I tried to stay with her, but then my job. . . . I tried to be there for her. But you know what? Some days I just couldn't face it any more, either. I gave her money."

"Sometimes you just can't help people no matter what," I said. "Why did she sign up for the summer class, I wonder?"

"I don't know," Debbie said. "Maybe it felt like a new start or something. She got some kind of financial assistance, even. God, if it hadn't been for that damn' Carl!"

Debbie looked at her watch and told me she needed to do some running around. She rose to go, then remembered something and sat down again. She dug in her purse and took out a large yellow envelope that she held onto while she studied my face.

"You really do want to help find her, don't you?" she asked. "I wasn't sure, but, for some reason, you seem really concerned about Cass. So I brought these for you, if you really want to get into this. I know you know what she looks like . . . but the cops on TV always have a picture to show people. They always say . . . 'Do you recognize this woman?' "

She put four photos on the table and lit up another cigarette while I studied them. One was a good head and shoulders shot of Cass Deering, one showed her with a young man, blonde and sort of fragile-looking, and the other two were of two very young girls and an older man standing beside a station wagon.

"Our dad," Debbie explained. "Mom took the picture. It's pretty good of Cass, except she's real young."

"New car?" I asked.

"That station wagon was Dad's pride and joy," Debbie

said, taking up the photo to look at it again. "It's a Nine-teen Seventy-Seven Ford Country Squire."

"I'm surprised you'd remember the year and model," I said, "since you were so young. I mean, I can remember a Chevy we had when I was ten or twelve, but sure couldn't tell you what year it was."

"With Dad you'd never forget! He told everybody he talked to about his Nineteen Seventy-Seven Ford Country Squire in showroom condition. He polished that car once a week. You know, he would even use little cotton swabs to clean inside the lettering on the side where it said Country Squire. Later on, at his funeral, some of his friends said Dad even thought of himself as a country squire. Dad talked like we were related to millionaires in California."

"*Those* Deerings?" I said. "The John Deere tractor family?"

"Yes. I think he always dreamed that one of his girls would marry into that family somehow. Then we'd be rich and drive around in our big cars to see how the poor folks were doing. He loved to do that on weekends, just cruise the roads waving to farmers in the fields, and waving to on-coming cars like he was the biggest cheese in the county."

"Did you go along?"

"Oh, we all did! Mom would dress up in her good hat. Cass and I would climb clear into the back of that big long wagon and play with our dolls. It had a really big ol' door in back and a seat facing backward, just right for little girls. I think it folded down to make a platform for hauling stuff? But we loved it when he made it into a seat and we could be 'way back there. It was so private, you know? Really snug."

Debbie got a faraway look and her voice took on a tone of sadness. "Cass really hated having to sell that old station wagon after Dad died, you know. Well, I did, too. But Cass especially. But we needed to, so we could keep the house."

"I think I've seen those big station wagons with the extra seat in back," I said.

She pointed to the back window of the vehicle in the photo. "Right there," she said. "Sometimes Cass or I would sneak into the garage, when it wasn't cold, and climb into the car to play dolls. It was so quiet and peaceful to be back there, especially in the garage where it was dark."

She rose again and I asked her if I could borrow the photos to copy. She slipped them back into the envelope to hand to me, and I thought of one last question.

"Hey, I nearly forgot," I said. "Professor Palmer said you like to read. Did Cass ever give you a novel, I mean recently? Maybe one of the ones we used in that class?"

"Oh, sure," she said. "She gave me one from class. But it was pretty used. It had lots of her notes in it. And part of it was missing. I never read it, but I sure got the message."

"What message was that?" I said.

"I'm a fast reader, faster than Cass. It's because I get impatient, I guess. And I always look at the end of a book, you know? I can get through it faster if I know how it's going to end. Cass always kids me about that. So, I think she had this novel with the last couple of chapters missing and gave it to me like a kind of joke. You know, to kid me about my bad habit of reading the last chapters first. She was like that."

Debbie Deering gathered up her pack of cigarettes and put them into her denim purse, which she put on top of the basket of folded laundry.

"What book was it?" I asked.

"*Madame Bovary*," she said.

Walking back to the truck with the summer heat on my back, I thought about that book. I didn't know much about

Debbie Deering, but Emma Bovary led a pretty wild life and got herself in trouble fooling around with a lover while she was married. There was no way I was going to dig into Debbie Deering's life, but, if the pattern held true, it was reasonable to assume that Cass had once again tried to use one of the books from my list to convince someone she cared about—her sister, in this case—that fiction imitates life and predicts the outcome of your decisions.

This time Cass had tried to soften the lesson. She had pulled back from the final horrific result of Emma Bovary's adulteries, not wanting Debbie to know Emma's final solution to her troubles. In the chapters Cass tore out of Flaubert's novel, Emma Bovary swallows arsenic. But Debbie seemed much stronger and at ease with herself and the life she had chosen. I wasn't at all worried about Debbie.

And the questions were still with me as I drove back toward Alliance: Did Cass Deering see *herself* in one of the novels she read, and, if so, which one? And when did she realize it? Did she stab Carl and then say . . . "Oh, my God, it's just like in that book!" Or did she see the connection long before that?

I passed a deserted farmhouse sitting back off the two-lane highway. The sight of it reminded me of another deserted house, an abandoned house in one of the novels. Suddenly a whole scenario began to play out in my mind. If Cass saw herself in . . . ? If she recognized the parallel . . . ? If. If. *If.* In theory, at least, it was a scary possibility. *If* she and I had the same book in mind, and it was a big if, then I might know where to start looking.

Chapter Eight

"I wasn't interested in the pots of gold he kept saying were just over the next hill, I went because there was a story to write. . . . A writer has to follow a story if it leads him to hell itself. That's our curse. Ay, and each one of us knows our own private hell. . . . A writer's job is to find and follow people like Justino. They're the source of life."
    "B. Traven Is Alive and Well in Cuernavaca"
        in *The Silence of the Llano*
            —Rudolfo A. Anaya

One more week of class to go and I was more impatient than the students. I managed to get in touch with Aggie on her cell phone, while she was somewhere between Milwaukee and Boulder, to let her know I was thinking of staying on in Alliance another week or two to "wrap things up." Her reaction was suspicion, but not the kind you're thinking of. Aggie knows only too well that her husband has a habit of getting too involved in what she calls his "little adventures" and losing track of his schedule. However, she said, she probably wouldn't be very good company for me if I did come home, what with her whirlwind of meetings concerning the new fund-raising effort.

"Fund-raising?" I said. "What are they raising funds for this time?"

"The library."

"I thought that project was dead."

"It was . . . but would you believe it? . . . I don't know how I got so lucky! Senator Burskin found a wealthy alum who wants to be remembered with a *wing* in the library. A whole *wing*, David! If I can just get the right ducks lined up, this will put the whole funding process back on track."

I wished her luck. And I thanked my lucky stars I wouldn't be available to help coerce those waterfowl into line. I spend enough of my time, during the regular school year, wearing a dark suit to cocktail parties so I can listen to alumni wives talk about grandchildren while Aggie plies the husbands with tales of woe about building permits and soil tests and eco-issues. For now, I had a theory about a missing person and perhaps even the murder of Carl Deerfield. And in a week I would have time to follow it.

At the police station Bob Houghton was watching Ronnie Webber fill out a form. Ronnie was working for Dale's Garage again, driving the wrecker part time.

"OK," Houghton said, taking the paper. "I'll get a copy of this made and send it to Dale." He put it in the basket marked **Accident Reports**.

"Have an accident?" I asked.

"No way," Ronnie sneered. "I cleaned one up last night. Took an hour t'get one car out from under the bridge."

"What can I do for you, Doc?" Sergeant Houghton asked.

"I went to Morris yesterday," I said, "and talked with Debbie Deering. She gave me some pictures of her sister, and I was thinking of driving around and showing them to people. Maybe I'll snoop in a few places."

I put my enlargements on the counter for him to look at. The do-it-yourself photocopier at the drugstore did a good job of enlarging them.

"OK with me," he said. "That's a good picture of her. That one in front of the station wagon is pretty old, though. She was just a kid. Debbie showed me these before."

"Bob," I said, "all this stuff about cars got me to thinking. We probably know what kind of car she drove, right?"

"That'd be an 'Eighty-Nine Fairlane, silver blue. A four-door," Ronnie volunteered.

"The kid never forgets a car," Bob said.

"Did she always use the same filling station?"

"I checked that. She always went to Dale's garage. In a small town like this, you generally stick to one place. Most of us do, anyway. What's your point?"

"Just that she supposedly took off in the middle of the night after the murder. Everything would have been closed up, right? And you probably asked nearly everybody in town if they saw her, including the filling station?"

"Right. If you mean did she stop at Dale's for gas, the answer is no."

"OK. But what I want to know is when was the last time she *did* gas up? In other words, could we figure out how far she might have gone before she had to stop for gas?"

Houghton leaned back in his chair and pondered my supposition. He got up and walked around the counter to look at a map of the Nebraska panhandle taking up most of the back wall of the station. A thumbtack stuck in the map marked Alliance, and attached to the tack was a measuring tape marked in miles.

"Penny!" he called out. "Get Dale on the phone, will you?"

In a few minutes, we had even more information than I had hoped for. It seems Cass Deering was a young woman of habit. Dale said she always filled up on pay day, and by then was almost always running on empty. He saw her every two weeks, like clockwork. The night she took off for parts unknown was the day before she would have gone to the gas station, and Dale figured her tank was nearly dry, unless she had filled up somewhere else. He also knew she didn't trust her gas gauge. She used her odometer to tell her when she was about out of gas, and had told him she got around 250 miles to the tankful.

"Ronnie," Sergeant Houghton said, "if she had less than a quarter of a tank of gas, how far could she go before she had to fill up?"

Ronnie did some math on the police blotter. "Probably actually got about three hundred miles to a tank. Let's see . . . what's a quarter of that?" He fiddled around with the pencil. "Seventy-five miles. That'd get her to Scottsbluff or Sidney. Or maybe Kimball. If she went north, she might make it to Chadron."

"But according to Dale, she's figuring her fuel according to her odometer," I suggested. "She'd be getting nervous and would be looking for an all-night station. Maybe . . . just maybe . . . somebody working at an all-night gas station within sixty miles of here remembers seeing her. It might be worthwhile to take a drive and ask."

It sounded like a big project, but in reality it wasn't as ambitious as it sounds. Only three highways lead out of Alliance, or four if you count the two parallel ones running north, and there couldn't be more than a dozen all-night places within sixty miles. The big question was whether anyone would remember a young woman in an older Ford Fairlane with a sickly-looking guy as a passenger. A long shot. Still, you never know. Cass or Michael may have done something or said something that would stick in a cashier's memory.

"Can't afford to spare anybody," Sergeant Houghton said, "but I tell you what I'll do. I'll give Penny the particulars and she can phone the truck stops and convenience stores within a sixty or seventy mile circle. There aren't any east of here on Highway Two, so she could concentrate on Chadron and Bridgeport first."

"You buy me a couple of tanks of gas and I'll start drivin' around and ask," Ronnie offered.

He was in luck—I had just picked up my summer teaching check and I was feeling pretty flush. "You got it," I said. I fished three twenties out of my wallet and gave them to him. "To start with, why don't you run down towards Bridgeport and look for late-night or all-night stations?"

I looked at the pictures. "Too bad we don't have a picture of her car, too," I said.

Ronnie looked at the picture that showed the two girls and their father standing by the station wagon. "That's a 'Seventy-Seven Country Squire," he announced. "There's one of them out at Carhenge, just like that one. In fact, there's two wagons together, only the other one's a Town 'n' Country. Might be a 'Seventy-Eight. They're right next to the death car. Well, I gotta go get the wrecker back t'Dale's."

Bob went into Penny's office to tell her what we were up to. I stood looking at the map. Which way did Cass Deering go when she left Alliance? Highway 385, south toward Bridgeport, was one choice, except I thought she knew people in that direction and people knew her. She was trying to get away, away from everyone. She wouldn't have run toward relatives and friends in the Scottsbluff area. Too many people in that direction.

East, then, out lonely Highway 2? If she were worried about gasoline, she wouldn't have gone down that road, or, at least, not very far. If she kept going out east on Highway 2, the car would have been found abandoned or somebody would have reported stopping to help her—and Michael? Was he with her on that road?

North seemed the most logical direction.

Bob Houghton came back to the desk. "All set," he said. "The trail's pretty cold, of course, but you never know what a few phone calls can turn up. Good luck, Doc."

"I'm going to drive north, I guess," I said. "Up Highway Eighty-Seven. What did the kid mean about a *death* car?"

"Local legend. Something else to get me out of bed at night, checking out calls from nervous citizens. Legend has it a woman committed suicide in that car. Drove out into the sand hills, somewhere, and hooked up a hose to the exhaust pipe."

"And did she?"

"Hell, I don't know! All I know is what the story says. It happened a long time ago. Anyway, it was summer and they didn't find her for weeks. They say the smell of death got into the metal and everything. Supposedly somebody bought the car and it started to stink when the weather warmed up, and so they sold it, then the next guy and the next guy had the same experience. Some people tell it that one buyer even replaced the seats, headliner, and everything, and the smell was still there. And people swore the car would moan at night, too.

"Finally everybody decided it was haunted," he went on, "so it was junked and ended up in Carhenge, so the story goes. Once in a while somebody hears wind blowing through the place or some stray dog howling, and then calls me at midnight to go out and see if there's a ghost in the death car." Bob shook his head, exasperated at the whole waste of his time.

"More night noises out there," I said. "I didn't realize it was such a spooky place."

"Yeah," Bob said. "Well, Doc, I got papers to shuffle. See you later?"

"You bet," I said. "Oh, just a minute. I really came in to see if you'd give me one or two of your business cards. If I get crosswise with a landowner or somebody, maybe I could show them your card and tell them you'd vouch for me."

"No problem," Bob said, handing me a half dozen cards from a little rack on the counter. "Say, I nearly forgot! It's Edna's birthday tomorrow and we're throwing her a party over at Ed's bar. Come on over. About eight?"

"Sure. See you."

When I climbed into the truck cab, fastened my seatbelt, and put on my sunglasses, Horse snorted and roared to life like he thought we were about to burn up the road, but he would have to wait a bit. First, we drove to Mrs. Samuels's house, the murder site where Cass was last seen. Perhaps by Ronnie Webber.

Mrs. Samuels's car was gone, which was good; I wouldn't have to answer any questions. I pulled around to the back alley and parked in the same narrow gravel strip where Cass would have parked her '89 Fairlane. *OK, I thought. Now I'm her. Been living with this creep for quite a while, and then this other man . . . my husband? . . . shows up in town, and he's sick and needs me. Maybe I thought he was dead, or had left me forever. Anyway, I want to end this thing with Carl, so there's a fight with him about my leaving. Big fight. He hits me. I grab the kitchen knife and stab at him, and it goes clear in. Shock. Horror. Then confusion.*

My main thought is to get away. I feel like Mrs. Samuels knows my every move and has probably heard the commotion, and Ronnie is always trying to look in the windows or watching me when I'm outside. I just need to get away from all the eyes. I need to be alone. No, I want to be with Michael. Let's see . . . he's at the motel, other side of town. Do I phone him? He's on foot, no car. Arrived in town on the bus.

I wondered if the cops found any blood on the telephone to show that she had used it after the murder, to see if she'd called anyone. I looked up at the door of the apartment over the garage and imagined it opening, imagined Cass Deering wearing whatever she had thrown on, coming out the door, slamming it, standing on the wooden landing, looking around with wild eyes, running down the steep wooden stairs, getting into her four-door Ford parked right here.

She'd take the car and go get Michael! That's exactly what she'd do.

I backed Horse out of the parking place and followed what I figured was her route through the alley, the quickest way to the street that would lead out to the motel on Highway 2. I imagined a dark night, Cass fearfully looking right and left in case anyone was out there to see her. She probably wouldn't know if Carl was dead or not. She sure wouldn't wait around for him to die. She's running from everything, not just murder. Just everything.

I could see the tall sign for the motel about six blocks away, and in my imagination I saw a skinny, sickly man coming up the sidewalk as fast as he could, waving at her car, stopping her. It's Michael. She phoned him, maybe told him what she'd done, and he jammed his stuff into a bag and rushed out to meet her. Probably didn't want her pulling into the motel where she might be seen. He gets into her car . . . just about here, I decided, pulling to the curb. And from here which way would they go? . . . ah! On my left, a diagonal street looked like it would lead back toward

Highway 87. I took that street and found myself on the highway. I pulled off into the parking lot of the auto parts store and unfolded my Nebraska road map.

Highway 87 goes straight north past Carhenge for about sixteen miles. There it comes to an intersection. Turn west, six miles or so, and you hit Highway 385 leading to Chadron. Stay on the highway as it does a forty-five-degree bend to the northeast and you find yourself headed for the sand hills and pine ridge country. Late at night it's as lonely as anyone could want. But there would be a gas station open once you got to Chadron.

The implications were obvious. Either she had made it to Chadron to get gas or she had been forced to ditch the Ford on some lonely side road along the way. According to my theory, those were the only two options, and they made the search seem simple. I put the pickup in gear and hit my turn signal to get back on the highway.

"Let's go look for a car, Horse," I said, my skin prickling with anticipation.

Horse and I drove north slowly, watching both sides of the road for a car. But before long I realized why we wouldn't find it. It had been more than a year, so any car that ran out of gas on this road would long, long ago have been towed away. I realized something else, however—it wasn't the car that really mattered. What I was hoping to discover was a spot that *felt* right. I hoped to come to a place where I could visualize her car pulling off the road. Maybe it would be a farm road, two ruts grown over with weeds. Maybe a dirt track leading down into a creek bottom. Maybe a grass-covered old driveway leading into an abandoned shed.

I was waiting for the *feeling*. I was looking for it to kick in and convince me I was driving the same route as Cass

Deering. The *feeling* has happened to me enough times that I'm a believer in it. Sometimes, when I'm out on what Aggie somewhat condescendingly calls my "little adventures" and I'm following the route of some long-dead writer in hopes of coming across a forgotten site or an old manuscript, the *feeling* tells me when the trail is the right one. Sometimes I get the right sensation. Sometimes I get something else, a sense of certainty that I'm in the wrong place.

People have asked me what it's like, and all I can say is having the *feeling* is like suddenly being aware of a kind of invisible current, as if there had been people moving around and doing things, then they went away but their energy fields stayed there and kept right on with what they had been doing. When it happens the other way around, it feels like more than nothing. It feels devoid of any energy. Take that Italian garden, for instance, where Lord Byron, the English poet, supposedly used a wooden gate for target practice. I stood where he would have stood, and I felt immediately that no one had been there shooting a pistol. There was a kind of hole in the air, a kind of vacuum where the energy should have been.

The highway leading up toward the sand hills didn't trigger the *feeling,* but it still felt vaguely right. I drove all the way to Hay Springs, where the highway going north comes to an end against an east/west highway. I went a few miles east, then a few miles west. Nothing. No hole in the air and no *feeling,* either. My gut told me Cass had driven the highway going north and that something had happened along the way. It also told me she hadn't made it to Chadron.

Back in Alliance that afternoon, I went to the library to look through their archive of magazines going back to the 'Sixties. It didn't take long to find a 1989 issue of *Popular*

114

Science with a full-color ad for the 1989 Ford Fairlane. The car in the picture was red, but a small inset picture showed a silver blue four-door just like Cass Deering's. I talked the librarian into using her color copier to make me a couple of copies and left the library whistling a little tune, feeling like I was one of those gumshoe private eyes in a Nero Wolfe novel.

Much to Horse's delight we spent the remaining daylight on the road, driving east on Highway 2. It didn't give me any of the *feeling*, but I wanted to explore all the possibilities. Horse particularly enjoyed it when we turned onto a gravel road running north into the sand hills lake district. On the bumps and washboards the spare tire bounced around in the bed, the loose tools skated back and forth in the toolbox, and the jack under the seat banged away happily. With no weight in the rear and three-quarter-ton suspension, the only way I kept control of the truck was to stay under forty miles per hour, and even at that we skidded on corners where the tires broke traction. Horse wiggled his rear end from side to side like a spastic conga dancer.

Every once in a while I spotted an old wreck in a wooded draw or half buried on an exposed slope, but never the one I wanted. We found a blacktop road and drove as far as the Niobrara River, but with all the haystacks we saw, we didn't see a single sign of the needle that might sew up the Cass Deering case. After dark we came cruising back into Alliance with Horse's fuel gauge reading "panic". Time to gas up at the Sand Hills Farmer Convenience Store, get a juicy burger from the A&W, and head over to the Homesteader for a bedtime beer. The evening was relatively cool; the air was quiet. A few kids cruised the street in their cars and a few couples strolled the sidewalks, looking in the windows of closed shops.

"Quiet tonight," I said to Ed as he brought me my beer. *And lonely,* I thought as he left me to drink by myself.

The next day I took my dirty clothes to the Laundromat, and, while it went through the tumbling, rinsing, and drying and all that, I sat and doodled in my notebook about the case. There were so many parallels between the novel and Cass's situation it actually began to worry me. I was afraid I was about to leap to conclusions that would make me bend facts to fit my theory. I needed to slow down and review other books on the list and experiment with other possibilities.

I would stay inside the one big theory, namely that Cass Deering had seen her own life in one of the novels named after women. Everything I'd seen so far pointed to a pattern: She couldn't help seeing parallels between real life and fiction, and she couldn't keep herself from trying to do something about it.

The broadest possible outline of her own story is that her father is dead and she tries to support the family, but she gets seduced and pregnant. In *those* terms her story resembles a novel that hasn't yet surfaced as one of Cass's give-aways—*My Ántonia* by Willa Cather. Cather wanted it pronounced Bohemian fashion: Áhn'-ton-ee-ah. Ántonia's father commits suicide, she goes into town to work for a wealthy family, gets seduced and pregnant by what's-his-name, the bad guy. Cutter. Cutter shoots his wife and then shoots himself, making sure she's dead first so her family can't inherit his money.

That raised a question, but only for a moment. Could Carl have committed suicide somehow? I guess Bob Houghton would have looked into that, but it's hard to imagine this particular man shoving a butcher knife into his own chest. Let's fast-forward to the end of the novel, where Ántonia ends up marrying a farmer and having a pack of kids.

Maybe . . . maybe, I thought, *Cass Deering and Michael ended up in some obscure place out of state and they got farm jobs as tenants and settled down to live under an alias.* The problem with this theory, however, is that she would be compelled to let her sister know that she was alive and well. An even bigger problem is figuring out why Cass would continue following the plot of *My Ántonia* after she had killed Carl.

And then there's the disappearance of her car. Even if she had made it to a gas station, and then had driven to some faraway town, the car should have turned up eventually on somebody's records. If Cass and Michael had kept it, they would have had to renew the license once a year. If they had sold it, somebody else would have had to register it. If they had junked it, the junkyard Internet web would have to have a record of it. Bob Houghton would have the resources—and the resourcefulness—to find it.

None of Cass's friends had said anything about *My Ántonia,* so I was pretty sure that wasn't the novel in which she had seen herself. I thought about the list I had sent to Cass, not the one I eventually used in class, but a preliminary one that listed other titles. Helen Hunt Jackson's *Ramona* had been on that list, mostly for its historical interest. I wondered if Cass had read it. Even so, she probably wouldn't have identified with a half-breed girl who elopes with an Indian. And he—the Indian—gets hounded to death by the whites in the novel. No parallels with the Deering case.

My Ántonia would still bear looking into. I put my clean laundry back in the cardboard box that served as laundry basket, clean clothes hamper, coffee table, and doorstop in the trailer, put the box in the truck, and went back toward the library to get a copy of Cather's novel.

Driving past the Homesteader, I saw Ronnie Webber's little toy truck parked outside, and I decided to go in and see what he had found, if anything. I parked my pickup right next to his and sensed Horse wasn't much impressed with it. He seemed to be looking down on the import with considerable disdain. A Dodge can be *such* a snob sometimes, particularly an old Dodge.

Ronnie was at the bar, presumably drinking up the rest of my $60. I joined him, and Ed joined both of us, bringing me an icy cold mug of Bud.

"Find out anything?" I asked.

"Nope," Ronnie replied. "Bridgeport, Scottsbluff, Gering, nothing. I was goin' to go all the way to Mitchell, except the guy at Gering volunteered to call around for me, instead. Diamond Shamrock stations have a toll-free connection to each other."

"Too bad nobody saw her," I said. "I really thought we had a good idea there, about running out of gas. But it was a long shot that someone would remember a car from a year ago."

"You want me t'go t'Kimball, or maybe Sidney? I can get the time off from Dale."

"No," I told Ronnie. "I don't think she went that way. Or, at least, not that far, not without having to stop and get gas. What about junkyards? Or used car lots? Are you sure you and Sergeant Houghton got them all?"

"Bob's thorough, I'll say that for him," Ed put in.

"Man, you got that right," Ronnie muttered. "He's got every salvage yard in the Ewe-nighted States on that damn' network of his. You try to sell a stolen carb or trannie somewhere, Houghton, he knows about it."

"Which is why you do some of your buying out at Carhenge." Ed smiled.

"Damn' straight," Ronnie replied.

Ed suddenly quit wiping at the already clean bar and straightened up as if he had just remembered something. "Hey! What about those ol' boys up by Hay Springs? You suppose Bob checked with them?"

Thinking it was time to inject some logic into this conversation, I started to point out that there was really no reason to think Cass Deering would have dropped her car off at a junkyard, or sold it at one. I had only brought up the possibility because it was one thing that happens to cars, that's all. Some become part of something like Carhenge or end up as rip-rap on some riverbank, but most cars go to a junkyard in the end.

"Right, Doc," Ronnie said, his mind obviously spinning like a busted clutch. "But you know what, those ol' boys don't have no telephone or nuthin'. They're sure as hell not on no computer network. They don't even give receipts. Just a couple of old bachelor codgers scrapin' out a living sellin' used car parts."

"These old boys," I said. "Where exactly is their place? Maybe I'll run up that way tomorrow." I remembered Hay Springs. The *feeling* had faded out on me just south of there, and somehow I knew—or sensed—I was no longer on the route where Cass and Michael had been.

"Y'gotta look hard for it," Ronnie said, and Ed nodded in agreement. "What you do is you come down this hill, and there's a bridge over the Niobrara. Go another couple of miles. . . ."

Ed interrupted. "You'll never see it," he said. "It's 'way back off the road."

"If y'get to the turn-off to that lake, Walgreen or Walgrin or somethin' like that, you're too far," Ronnie continued. "Thing t'look for is the mailbox."

"Oh, yeah!" Ed laughed. "I'd forgot about that damn' mailbox."

"It's a huge ol' tractor muffler," Ronnie said, "sittin' on top a transmission case out of a diesel. You turn there, and their junkyard is back over the first hill. Can't see it from the highway."

"Should be easy enough to find," I said. "Near Hay Springs, then."

"South of there," Ed replied.

South, I repeated in my mind. South will do me fine.

Chapter Nine

The only thing very noticeable about Nebraska was that it was still, all day long, Nebraska. . . . There was nothing but land: not a country at all, but the material out of which countries are made. No, there was nothing but land, slightly undulating.

My Ántonia
—Willa Cather

Edna's friends had gone to a lot of trouble to decorate the Homesteader for her birthday party. I assumed it was a landmark birthday, her fortieth, or something like that. But I wasn't about to ask Edna how old she was; the next time I saw her, probably, she'd be holding a pot of scalding coffee over my lap to refill my cup.

Streamers and strips of crêpe paper were draped over Ed's illuminated beer signs, and three huge **Happy Birthday** banners were hung from wall to wall. Tables had been pushed together, surrounded with chairs, and covered with red and white paper tablecloths. Ed was busy taking brimming pitchers to each table, carrying stacks of plastic beer glasses tucked under his arm.

"I kinda wish you wouldn't carry my beer glass under your armpit, Ed," I greeted him.

"Hiya, Doc! Pull up a chair!" Ed had to yell over the noise of the George Strait tune bellowing out of a boom box. Three couples were doing their own interpretations of the Texas two-step on the postage-stamp-size dance floor.

121

Either that or they were just polishing each other's belt buckles in time to the music.

I helped myself to a beer, but, instead of pulling up a chair, I wandered to the end of the bar to sample the huge birthday cake. At the far end of the room, beyond the two pool tables, little kids were playing in a special area just for them. Somebody—Bob Houghton, probably—had donated a section of orange plastic fencing, the kind used at construction and accident sites. Other people had brought quilts and comforters and pillows galore, so the kids were all set in their own big, orange playpen. Two teenage girls supervised.

The trouble began while I was at the pool table watching a game of eight ball. One player suddenly took my plastic beer glass away from me just as I sensed someone else stepping up close behind me; before I knew what was happening, there was a pool cue pressed across my throat. I could tell that my assailant was shorter than me, but he had plenty of strength. He wasn't applying it, just keeping the pressure on. His chest was against my back, staying close where I couldn't reach back and get a hold on him.

He made no move, giving me time to take a few deep breaths and get myself centered. With each breath I forced a wave of relaxation down through my muscles. The guys around the table were grinning. In the light of the lamp hanging over the table I made out the thick end of the cue. My assailant had left a couple of feet of it sticking out. His wrists rested on my shoulders close to my neck.

That was his mistake. Hands too close together.

Your first impulse, when somebody has a stick across your neck, is to put both hands over your throat and push the stick away. But that position gives your forearms lousy leverage, like trying to do a push-up wearing handcuffs.

Instead, I reached with my left hand and got a grip on the butt of the cue stick, meanwhile using my right hand to clamp his hand to the stick. Then I twisted hard and fast, forcing the butt downward, then backward, then forward, twisting his trapped hand with it. Now he was the one who was in trouble; he was off balance and he couldn't bend his arm. He let go with the other hand, since his arm wouldn't stretch any further, but the movement only torqued his trapped arm like a wound-up rubber band on a model airplane.

The next move was simply a beginner's exercise. Using his own momentum to bring him alongside me, I stuck out my leg and braced it, and he sprawled over it to land on his back on the floor. He lost his grip on the cue stick, but it didn't fall to the floor because I now had it. A flip of my wrist brought it up to vertical and I stuck the thick end against his trachea.

"Hiya, Doc," he said carefully.

"Pat."

"We missed you at practice this summer. Been busy?"

"Yeah," I said, putting the stick on the table and helping him up. "Every summer it seems to take longer to grade papers and write lectures, you know?"

"Thought you professor types do everything on computers," Pat Kisimoto said. "But I seem to dump more paper than ever when I clean offices. Paper, paper, paper. Thank God for recycling, anyway."

"So who's in the group now?" I asked, taking my beer from the pool player who had rescued it when he saw Pat sneaking up on me. The other player took Pat's stick and put it in the rack, then went back to lining up his next shot.

"Oh, we got the same bunch. One of the kids who works for me, he's new. Gus, from the real estate office. Same crew. Only we got a new location."

"No more basement?" I said. Previous *bojutsu* workout sessions had taken place in a local church basement where the ceiling was so low we always hit it with our sticks.

"Gus got us an upstairs place, the big empty room over the Coast-to-Coast. It used to be a dance studio or something. Lots of space. Come and practice with us before you leave town."

I said I would, but didn't know if I could. I wandered toward the cake, and ran into Ronnie Webber, or should I say Ronnie ran into me. He seemed to have absorbed all the free beer he could hold. He looked like he would squish when he walked.

"Getting enough?" I said. "Who's paying for the beer, Bob Houghton?"

"That's what they say," he slurred. "Ashk me, I think he's tryin' t'get all of us drunk an' then, when we go t'leave he'll get us for drunk driving. Get his money back outta th' fines. Whatta ya think, Doc?"

"Sounds like a plan," I said.

I just about had a piece of cake to my mouth when one of my students bore down on me like a tugboat doing twelve knots. She was towing a woman I'd never seen before.

"Oh, Professor McIntyre!" she burbled. "I just have to tell you how much I loved the class. It was so good! I told my friend, Carla, here, about it, and told her she just has to take it next summer!"

"Hi." We shook hands, even though I had to put down my cake.

Karen—the tugboat—went on and on about Carla's interest in literature and how she hoped to get a teaching certificate herself someday. As the conversation droned around from one predictable topic to another, it unexpectedly came to Cass Deering. Again.

"Carla got a book from Cass Deering, you know."

"Really?" I said.

"Oh, yes. I told her you were interested in who Cass gave books to . . . well, you remember, after some of those talks we had in class about it . . . and she told me Cass gave her *My Ántonia*. By Cather, you know."

"I know the book." I turned to Carla. "Maybe we could find a quieter place. I'd like to ask you about it. How about over by the kiddie area? It seems to be quieter than the adultie area."

Karen took the hint and remained behind. I took a paper plate, put another piece of cake on it, and led the way to a little table on the far side of the pool tables.

"So Karen told you about Cass's penchant for giving novels to people," I said.

"Yes. Isn't it interesting? It's almost as though she sees herself as a character in some book or other. I mean it's like she's a heroine in a novel who goes around helping people by giving them books to read. Do you know what I mean?"

"Sure," I said. "That's just what I've been thinking my-self. So, she gave you *My Ántonia*? Any idea why she did that? That particular novel, I mean?"

"At first I didn't know," Carla admitted. "I just put it aside and ignored it for the longest time. Then one day I picked it up and found she'd made all kinds of notes in it, notes that seemed to be aimed at me particularly. I really don't want to talk about it . . . in fact, I've never told anyone before . . . but, well, I was raised on a farm and my parents died, and I moved into town and worked here and there. I had board and room with a family . . . well, that's the part I don't want to talk about. But Cass was right . . .

she sure saw what was going on with me."

"So the book helped?"

"I don't know as it helped, but it made me sort of see myself the way some outsiders would. I suppose in that way, it helped. The story made me feel much better, seeing how Ántonia ended up, happily married with kids and all."

"Hello, Professor." The new voice came out of the dim light of the pool table area. "Still hanging out in bars, I see."

Such a remark could only come from one person, and sure enough it was she. Hank. Henriette Palmer. In Western-cut jeans, shirt, and scuffed cowboy boots, she fit right in at the Homesteader birthday party.

"Professor Henriette Palmer, I'd like you to meet Carla . . . uh. . . ."

"Jakobson," Carla said. "Hi."

In case you haven't yet acquired a full picture of the attractive Professor Palmer, let me say that she only has to stand next to the Carla Jakobsons of the world and they seem to fade away. Within her aura, women do go on speaking and you might even listen to them, but they suddenly seem like background blurs in an Impressionist painting.

Carla Jakobson saw someone she wanted to say hello to and moved away. Hank and I walked back to the bar and stood sipping beer, tapping our toes to George Strait.

"You're surprised to see me," she stated. "But I need some advice."

"You drove all the way to Alliance to ask my advice?" I said.

"No, you arrogant truck driver. I drove into Alliance because I'm on my way to Lincoln. One of the editors at University of Nebraska Press wants to discuss publishing my dissertation. I thought I would pull one of your tricks and drive the whole way on two-lane blacktop, instead of using the interstate. There's so much more to see that way."

"You mean your book about the history of hotels in the West? I thought Oxford had first dibs on that one."

"Lachlan, you're not listening. As usual. I said dissertation, not book."

"What's it about?" As well as I knew Palmer, I guess I had never bothered to ask her what she had studied in graduate school. Or she had told me and I had forgotten.

"I've told you before. Early travel guides to the Great Plains."

"Oh, yes! We talked about Mason Peck's guide once upon a time. So, are you going to hang around a while, see old friends, come over to my trailer for a gin and tussle?"

"Yes, and definitely no. In fact, I'm going to have lunch with Doctor Venirs."

"Angling for another summer job, are you?"

"No. This is just for old time's sake. Unlike your habit of burning personal bridges behind you, I prefer to keep mine in good repair."

I didn't believe her. I figured she was lining up a summer appointment for some friend of hers back in Boulder, probably female. Dancers twirled past us, people recognized Hank and came to say hello, and Ed kept the pitchers of draft beer coming. Edna unwrapped her presents, we all sang the "Happy Birthday to you" song, even though it sounded like a chorus of vocally impaired livestock at feeding time, and one by one the little kids curled up in the quilts at the back of the room and went to sleep. The evening was grinding to a close.

I walked Hank out to her car. I even opened the door for her. "Hey," I said. "I just had an idea."

"First time for you?" She smiled sweetly, slipping her keys out of her purse.

"I need to go interview a couple of old bachelor hermits at their wrecking yard tomorrow, about the Cass Deering disappearance. Want to come along?"

"Golly," she said, "another date among junked cars, and this time with three old geezers at once. How can I refuse? What's your angle, Lachlan?"

"I'll tell you mine if you tell me yours."

"Mine?"

"About coming out here. You're really here to talk Venirs into hiring some pal of yours from back home, right?"

"Wrong. I hate to admit it, but I did want your advice. You're *so* much older and more experienced." That was a blatant bit of perjury. She and I are within a few days of being the same age. And we won't go into "experience".

"OK," I said, somewhat disarmed by her admission she wanted my advice. "I guess I have an angle, if you want to call it that. Sometimes these old-timers can be hard to approach, especially for an out-of-towner like me. But if you went along, kind of like we were a couple, it might soften them up."

"I know what you want, Lachlan," she teased, "and it's nothing to do with softening anybody up."

"Sure it is. C'mon. I'll pack a lunch, we'll have a nice drive, and it'll be fun."

To my everlasting surprise, she agreed. She not only agreed, but she didn't even object to driving out there in Horse. It would be uncomfortable, without air conditioning, but I thought maybe a vintage pickup would make a better impression in a junkyard than the Buick. So setting out the following day with wine and sandwiches and fruit on ice in the Styrofoam cooler bungee-corded to the spare tire, we rode north up Highway 87 looking for a mailbox made from a muffler mounted on a transmission housing.

My colleague took full advantage of the situation to pursue her purpose, even though she almost had to shout— with the windows open, the truck makes a lot of noise.

"About this conversation with Nebraska Press," she said. "If you were my chairman, or if you were hiring me at another school, would you be impressed that I had published my dissertation, or would you think I should have spent my time doing something more timely, more relevant? I don't want to spend a year polishing this thing just to have it be a little blip on my resumé. Besides, I'm not as interested in the topic as I used to be."

"We all have that problem," I said above the roar of wind. "You also need to factor in the point that neither your chairman, nor a chairman looking to hire you, would actually sit down and read your book. It'll only be a line on your curriculum *vitæ*, that's all. Some hiring committee will look at your *vitæ*, count the number of publications you have, and decide whether to interview you."

"You're a real boost to the ego, you know that?"

"You also need to consider whether you have enough interest in the subject to spend all that time getting it ready for publication," I said.

"I really enjoyed the research," Hank said. "I spent nearly a year reading old pioneer guidebooks and going out to look at the various sites they had described. One book, written by a woman, had a very moving passage about standing on a high hill looking out onto the Great Plains. After I read it, I was standing on top of Scotts Bluff trying to imagine what it all looked like when it was empty. For a few moments I actually felt like I was standing beside a covered wagon, seeing into the future."

"Pretty common experience!" I shouted over the wind roar. "Good books are supposed to affect the emotions like that. Well-written books, I mean. That's what I'm finding out as I talk to people Cass Deering gave books to. She might have stood beside her car out here somewhere and seen herself as someone like Jane Eyre."

"Jane Eyre? Why Jane Eyre?" Hank asked.

I slowed down to forty so we could talk without yelling.

"Well," I said, "you remember that scene when she leaves Rochester's house and flees into the night, don't you? She's confused, distraught, out of her mind with emotional pain. She runs away, and all she can think of doing is to get far away from his house to throw herself down in the heath and trust Mother Nature to preserve her."

"And you think Cass did what? Drove to some remote spot and threw herself down in the heath, or whatever passes for heath in Nebraska? Then what? I suppose you're going to tell me she died of exposure out there, in mid-summer."

"Don't laugh. It can happen. You go without food long enough, get dehydrated, go through a few adrenaline attacks, you can die of exposure in fifty-degree nighttime temperatures. It doesn't even have to be that cold for hypothermia to get you."

"And is *Jane Eyre* your book of choice, then?"

"Not really. In fact, things are starting to fall into place that point to another novel. One I hadn't thought of until I heard about her father and his Country Squire. It's a novel by. . . ."

"There!" Hank interrupted. "There's your mailbox!"

Indeed it was. There was nothing in sight except a break in the barbed-wire fence, a narrow road leading around a low hill, and an oversize tractor muffler welded atop a transmission housing. Whoever welded it had made a hinged door out of one end, and left about a foot of tailpipe sticking out as a handle. It wasn't meant to be cute or artistic, just big, functional, and cheap. Years of sand hills sun and wind had long ago licked it clean of any name or address.

"That's a huge mailbox," Hank said. "They must get a lot of mail and packages."

I turned off the highway and we bounced along the twin ruts around the rise of prairie. And there it was, a sprawling quarter-section of rusty metal covering three hills and filling half a dozen gullies. We drove between combines from the Dust Bowl days, and pre-war tractors, unrecognizable bodies of delivery vans and milk trucks, piles of wheels and stacks of pickup beds. The ruts suddenly forked and we found ourselves in a dead-end, the way blocked by the remains of innumerable windmill towers and unidentifiable pieces of equipment twisted into grotesque sculptures. I backed up and took the other turn, muttering something about Robert Frost's "Road Less Traveled", and, after passing between two long rows of stacked car bodies ready to collapse, we came to the house.

House is a relative term, of course. On the sagging porch of the slightly tipsy two-story farmhouse two hulking mastiffs roused themselves and came toward the truck with half-hearted woofs of warning. I turned Horse around in the yard so Hank's door would be toward the dogs.

"Thanks," she said.

I spotted an old guy sitting on a bench under a shade tree by a garage that had also seen much better days. *Decades* of much better days.

Several minutes passed while we sat there with the heat

133

coming in through the open windows, waiting for somebody to come out or at least call off the dogs. Behind the dilapidated garage and sandblasted farmhouse, the plains of Nebraska rolled away in heat waves. Lazy streaks of shadow rose and fell with the hills, marking wooded gullies. Somewhere, farther east, the gently swelling hills give way to abrupt rocky bluffs cloaked in forests of pine. But as far as our eyes could see, there was only this unaccountably expansive yard of junk, two spiritless watchdogs, one grizzled junkman fossilizing on his bench, and us, sweltering in the steel cab.

The two dogs sat down in the shade of the truck. From time to time they looked up at Hank, looked over at the old man on the bench, growled half-heartedly, and blinked themselves back to sleep.

"Might as well do it," I said, opening the door and stepping out. I walked toward the garage, alert to the possible sound of eight feet and two slobbering mouths coming up behind me. When I made a pause to take a tentative look back, the ancient dogs were limping arthritically back toward the porch.

"Good morning!" I called out as cheerily as I could.

A second old man came hobbling out of the darkness of the garage.

"Ain't buyin' nuthin' "—he said, and, scowling in the direction of Horse—" 'specially no damn' ol' Dodge."

I forced a diplomatic good-ol'-boy laugh, as if he were joking. "That's a damn' good ol' Dodge," I said. "And I sure wouldn't sell it."

"You got thet damn' straight," said the other. "Not here, nohow. Piece of shit."

OK. Not a good start. Why the hell wasn't Hank coming over to back me up here? I went on to the next ploy, taking one of Sergeant Houghton's cards out of my shirt pocket. "Sergeant Houghton down in Alliance said you might help me." I smiled.

"Who?"

"Sergeant Houghton. Alliance?"

I heard the crunch of sandals on gravel and knew Hank was finally joining in. The shorter of the two geezers scratched at his gray stubble and hitched a thumb in the single unbroken strap holding up his coveralls.

"You know that son-of-a-bitch?" he said.

"Houghton? Uh, yeah."

"Ain't much of a lawman, is he?"

"Well," I stammered, "he, uh, I guess he's all right for a small town like Alliance." I held out the business card as if to justify my visit. The geezer on the bench got up, took it, and sat down, studying it. He handed it to the other one.

"Mean anythin' t'you, Bud?"

Bud returned it to me with greasy thumbprints on it. "What's it say?" he said.

What's it say? My God, these two may not only be mentally challenged, they're illiterate!

Hank took the card from me and read it to them. "Robert M. Houghton, Sergeant, City of Alliance Police Department, Two-Oh-Nine, Five-Five-Five, Two-One-Two-One. Fax . . . Two-Oh-Nine, Five-Five-Five, Two-One-Two-Four."

"Fucks?" Bud said.

"Facts, you dumb butt-hole," the other one said. "Y'telephone him there f'r facts."

"Got no phone."

Seeing that my interview was deteriorating faster than the car bodies out in their oxidizing junkyard, Professor

Palmer took charge. The first thing she did was to step over into the shade of the scraggy elm tree beside the garage, which forced the one on the bench to scoot around to face her. The other one leaned on the doorway, hands hanging by the thumbs from his coverall pockets.

"Now," Hank said. "My friend and I are looking for a car."

"Don't blame y', do we, Cliff? That Dodge is a piece of shit."

Cliff chortled. "And we don't take no trade-in Dodges," he said.

"No," Hank persisted, "we're looking for a car that may have been abandoned somewhere in this area, about a year ago. Lachlan, do you have that picture?"

I took out the folded photocopy.

"Looks like this," I said. "It's a Nineteen Eighty-Nine Ford Fairlane."

"No shit, Dick Tracy. And it sure ain't no damn' Dodge," Bud said.

"Not a Plymouth, neither," Cliff chortled. "Anythin' wors'n a Dodge is a Plymouth." He spat at his feet. And hit one of them.

They looked at the picture, leaving more greasy fingerprints on it, and I noticed the way Hank was looking around. There's this about her—when she starts really, really to look at things, she generally sees more than I do. This seemed to be one of those times. I saw her brow furrow above her aviator sunglasses, then saw her lips tighten thoughtfully. She looked at Bud, then at Cliff. She peered into the dark cavern of the garage. Finally she sat herself down on the bench next to Cliff.

"You knew Sergeant Houghton was looking for this car last year, didn't you?" she said in *that* tone of voice. It's the tone she uses when she catches a student cheating on an exam.

Cliff said nothing. Guilty.

"I'll bet he overlooked your . . . uh . . . automotive recycling center," Hank said.

"We calls it a junkyard," Bud said.

"And thet's puttin' it nice-like," Cliff added.

I wanted to jump in and ask them point-blank if they knew the car might be involved in a murder, and maybe even threaten them with bringing in the police to look around. But I waited. Hank seemed to have her own scenario.

"And doesn't a junkyard keep records of any kind? I'm interested in history, you see, and I find all kinds of interesting records people keep. Hotel registers, cargo lists, theater programs, all kinds of things. You gentlemen buy and sell used cars, trucks, and farm machinery. Almost everything you deal with has an identification number. Surely you have to keep records. Your customers would need serial numbers in order to get vehicle licenses."

"What if we couldn' read?" Bud grinned and showed a broken tooth. "Can't expect no ill-literate person to go keepin' no records."

"Gotcha there," Cliff said.

The professor aimed a double-barreled frown at him, then put on a sneaky smile as she reached out with her long manicured fingers and slipped them under the bib of Cliff's denim coveralls as if she were evaluating the quality of the cloth. "Then what," she said, holding him immobile with her eyes while drawing out a small notebook and stubby pencil from his shirt pocket, "do you do with *this?*" She opened the notebook, looked at it, then handed it to me. It contained lists of inventory, names, addresses, all in a neatly penciled hand.

"When did the JCPenney store close down in Alliance?" she asked Bud.

"I dunno. Few years ago. Why?"

"You're wearing Penney's overalls, and I'll bet they're less than a year old. Got them mail order, right?"

I couldn't hold back. "How the heck do you know that?" I said.

"Why else would they have such a big mailbox, except to get catalogs and mail-order packages? Shirts, coveralls, those work shoes, they're all catalog merchandise. Bud and Cliff are literate enough to order clothes by mail. OK, now, Bud. My friend and I don't really have all day. What's the story on this car in the picture?"

Bud grinned weakly. He liked this professor of history, he did. Heck, who wouldn't? But he wasn't going to give in, at least not just yet.

"I'll tell you what let's do, Bud," Hank Palmer went on, "let's play let's pretend. Let's pretend you found that car and didn't know who abandoned it. Then let's pretend Sergeant Houghton forgot to check your junkyard when he was looking for it. Then let's pretend you and good ol' Cliff here don't have a telephone and, golly, can't read! So the police department doesn't have any way of letting you know there's a car missing. Now, let's see. What is the law out here? Three years? After three years you can claim it? As long as no one finds it and claims it first?

"But let's pretend you really can read. Penney's or one of the other mail-order places might have copies of orders with your writing on them. Let's pretend you were sent a police flier about the car. Let's even pretend a cop came out here to tell you to watch for it. If you're hiding it, and somebody lets Sergeant Houghton know, you can bet your catalog work shoes he's going to come out here and look around every time anyone reports a car stolen. How about them apples, Bud?"

Bud laughed and shook his head at himself like a man who just let a woman beat him at checkers. He got up and shuffled into the garage. We followed him, and, after our eyes became accustomed to the gloom, we saw a roll-top desk and a steel filing cabinet. Bud opened a file drawer and flipped through folders until he found the one he was looking for.

"Here's Cliff's description of that 'Eighty-Nine Fairlane," he said, showing us a sheet of notebook paper. "It's still parked out there, if you want to look at it."

I assumed he was going to walk us through the wrecked car bodies, but instead he climbed onto the seat of an old Farmall tractor fitted with a front-end loader and motioned for us to follow him in the truck. He took us along dirt paths through a maze of junk piled precariously high on either side, until, at last, we came to a patch of grass where a dozen or more cars were parked. Unlike the relics elsewhere in the yard, these were intact under their layers of grime. One had a sun-bleached **For Sale** sign in the window.

Bud shut off his Farmall and climbed down.

"There she is," he said, pointing out a Ford sedan. "The story is, me an' Cliff, we don't talk all that much t'one another a good part of th' time. I come in here las' summer an' found that Ford sittin' there. Figured, y'know, Cliff, he bought 'er and put 'er there an' didn't write it down. Turns out he figured I'd done the same thing."

"Was the car just like this," I asked. "I mean did you move it? I hope you didn't mess up any fingerprints. That's evidence in a murder case."

"Found 'er sittin' there, left 'er sittin' there," Bud said.

"Th' tire tracks looked like somebody drove 'er in here off that ol' farm road over there."

"See anything else? Footprints? Something somebody might have dropped on the ground, other car tracks, broken fence, anything unusual?"

Bud mused. In fact, he mused so long I was afraid he'd gone off to sleep. But he finally spoke.

"Yeah," he said. "There was a trail. Th' dogs found 'er with me."

"Her?" Hank asked.

"The Ford," he said. "They was with me when we found 'er here. They sniffed at 'er doors, an' then they sniffed a beeline over t'that fence 'way out there. Ain't hard to figger that whoever parked 'er here went walkin' away in that direction. That's th' way I'd go, wouldn' you?" He was pointing due south at a sagging barbed-wire fence. "Then there's the gas cap thing."

"Gas cap thing?" Hank said.

"Yeah. OK, see that Chevy next t'the Ford? Found 'er gas cap on top of the Ford. An' somebody had the hood up on that other Ford over there, that two-door. We figured on it, after we figured that it wasn't me or him that bought 'er, and we figured some kids came drivin' in here lookin' for gas, like they was runnin' low. So they got in here and stopped next t'this Chevy and opened th' tank an' went lookin' for a piece of hose, like a heater hose maybe, then figured out they had 'er on the wrong side. See that?"

Sure enough. They had pulled in next to the Chevrolet wrong side; the gasoline filler opening was on the other side. Maybe there wasn't enough fuel in the Ford to get it started again and turn it around.

"Yep," I said. "Wrong side. But a siphon wouldn't work,

anyway, not from one car to another. They're level with each other."

"Your friend here's purty quick, ain't he?" Bud said to Hank.

"Oh, my, yes," she replied. "He's a college professor, you know."

I got my cell phone from Horse and called Sergeant Houghton to tell him we might have found the missing car, and he said he would come right away. Then Hank and I tried to learn what we could from looking at the car, without touching it, an activity that quickly bored our host. He mentioned some work he had to do and mounted his Farmall.

"Bud's probably anxious to tell Cliff the sergeant is coming," I said. "That was pretty good work you did back there, Professor! The mailbox stuff, the pencil and notebook, that speech you gave them."

"Nothing to it," she said. "I just noticed the bulge of the notebook and saw the end of the pencil sticking out and wondered why an illiterate junk flogger would carry a notebook. And when I looked at the house, I didn't see any sign of a television antenna or satellite dish, so it stands to reason that our two friends might spend their evenings reading magazines and mail-order catalogs. That's what made me think of the size of the mailbox."

While we waited for Bob Houghton, Palmer and I took turns guessing what happened next. Did the two young people run back to the highway? In the dark? Or, since the dogs seemed to have sniffed out a trace leading to the fence, did they walk cross-country, avoiding roads and houses?

We walked to the fence line. The country beyond the barbed wire looked so empty, so devoid of any kind of refuge. . . . Just across the fence, a field of wheat began with

141

an unwavering line of golden stalks and heavy heads, just like the next line and the next. They went on in perfect blond ranks until they seemed to merge into one level mass of wheat that rose and blended and flowed over the swelling of the hills until it seemed the earth itself had turned golden in the blaze of the sun.

On beyond the wheat, the hills fell away again to rise a mile farther on where they made a streak of dark green spreading from horizon to horizon. After that hill was another one of pale green and beyond that a far hill became the horizon and was darker yet. I climbed up onto one of the other cars, yelping as I touched the hot metal, and from that vantage point I was ready to swear I could see the entire curve of the prairie horizon. Two very small clouds hovered over the curve, staying close to each other for protection from the never-diminished sun.

"You know," I said when we were back in Horse's cab, "I think they headed that way, due south. Wish I had a topo."

"Topo?"

"Topographic map. Of the area. It shows the lines of elevation, location of roads and wells and windmills, that kind of stuff."

"I know what a topo map is, boy scout! What I meant was why do you want one?"

"Well," I said, "if I had a canteen and a topo map and a compass, I'd like to take off and follow their trail. Or what I think is their trail."

She gave me *that* laugh, the one that says I'm an idiot but she likes me anyway.

"Lachlan"—she smiled—"you're such a fuss. If they went that way in the dark without a map or compass, why can't you?"

"Good point." I was getting a tingle up my spine just thinking about making a cross-country trek in the starlight.

"I'll tell you what," Hank taunted me. "I'll drive you up here tonight, drop you off, and we'll agree on some place where I can pick you up in the morning. You go stumbling and tripping through the wheat and weeds, get shot at by farmers, meet hostile canines, and fall into ravines, while I relax in a bubble bath with a glass of white wine."

"I think I'll do just that," I said. "But why the bubble bath and wine?"

"Well, my dear Lachlan, I'm going to have such a good time thinking about you out here with the sandburs and snakes and shotguns! It's only fair you should have a nice time, too, thinking about me soaking in a bubble bath. Don't you agree?"

Lovely woman. No, really. She is. There I was, sitting in this oven of a truck cab, looking at a woman really worth looking at, and seeing behind her, out the truck window, those undulating soft hills with their yawning, gaping gullies of undergrowth, the golden wheat fading toward the horizon into soft blond fuzz. And the little tingle of adrenaline I was feeling was coming from the idea of walking across all that landscape.

No doubt about it, Lachlan, a little voice inside me said, *there's something seriously wrong with you.*

Chapter Ten

I knew not what to determine upon; my reputation now, no doubt, utterly ruined; destitute of clothes; unfit to be seen by anybody: my very indigence, as I might call it, proclaiming my folly to every one who saw me.

Clarissa
—Samuel Richardson

Never let it be said that Professor Henriette Palmer is not a good sport. She showed up at the trailer at 2:00 a.m., cheerful and cheery as could be, ready to do her share. Or ready to make certain I went through with my "idea". Whenever she referred to my "idea", it sounded like she was putting it in quotation marks like that.

Through the quiet semidarkness we drove back out to the junkyard, feeling like a couple of fugitives ourselves. There's something about cruising around at that strange hour that makes you feel sneaky or guilty of something. When a car came toward us on the lonely highway, I felt like scrunching down behind the steering wheel so they wouldn't see me.

Hank hummed a little tune to herself as we drove along and I fussed around with my thoughts. My primary thought was that I wasn't all that eager to go through with this idea of hiking across the fields and hills and gullies following a vague feeling. I was not as confident of my theory as I had been the previous afternoon. Complicating the issue was a

144

problem I am very, very familiar with, namely that I habitually worry away my initial excitement in such situations, and then find myself raising all kinds of neurotic barriers.

The whole idea seemed like a waste of time. On the other hand, it was just barely possible that Cass Deering *did* fall back on the novel as a last resort. Timing was the crucial factor: *If* she had realized the parallel, when did she realize it? And what was her state of mind? In my theory—the theory that was looking less and less plausible in the pre-dawn darkness—she had fled from town, taking Michael along, had run out of gas about this time of morning, and become uncertain what to do next. Close to panic and losing her hold on reality like a climber feeling the rope slipping through her failing fingers, she had seen herself as a character in a novel, a character who had gone through a very similar crisis. It may have happened at the junkyard, or somewhere much closer to town, but I believed that somewhere along their flight, she had ceased to be Cass Deering and become the protagonist in her novel, doing everything her protagonist had done. Given the trauma she had been through, it may have been the only pattern her mind could grasp.

Cass had annotated half a dozen novels she thought would help other women get perspective on their situations. If she had seen herself in the novel I was thinking of—and I was so uncertain of it that I didn't even share my suspicion with Hank—the ending would not have been a happy one for her.

By the time we came to the narrow old farm road, the back way into the junkyard, I was almost ready to drive back to town and forget the whole thing. Maybe I just didn't want to find any more parallels.

Truth to tell, the literary connection interested me as

much as the mystery of her disappearance, which meant my
logic and conclusions were biased in favor of finding the fictional parallel. In other words, I would keep finding literary
parallels because I *wanted* to find literary parallels. It was a
self-serving game; I was ready to follow any blind alley or
false lead so long as it kept the game going.

On the positive side, there was the small consolation that
only two other people—Bob Houghton and Henriette
Palmer—would know I had made a fool of myself when my
hypothesis laid a great big goose egg. The darker consolation was that, if the hypothesis was wrong, there might not
be a tragic conclusion to the Cass Deering story, after all.

Down the farm road we came to the dim track leading
into the junkyard, where I shut off the headlights and crept
forward in low gear. No need to wake up Bud and Cliff and
their geriatric canines. Horse sat in the dark little clearing,
the rumbling of the exhaust pipe echoing back from the sur-
rounding stacks of junked cars. I turned on the parking
lights to illuminate the opening between the derelict car
bodies and the sagging barbed-wire fence beyond.

I got out and Professor Palmer slid behind Horse's big
steering wheel. I took my walking stick and day pack from
the truck bed and slammed the door with a clang.

Hank rolled down the window. "No flashlight?" she said.
"No compass, no map?"

"If Cass and her Michael went this way, it was about as
dark as this. And they didn't have anything with them. At
least I've got a walking stick and canteen and something to
eat. And a cell phone!" I tapped the outside pocket of the
pack to make sure.

"So you'll call me when you're ready to be picked up,"
she said.

"Yep," I said, "probably mid-afternoon. Be sure to leave

your phone turned on! Now, are you absolutely sure you can handle Horse? Have you driven a five-speed stick shift? He can be pretty damn' obnoxious, especially with strangers. Might have to double-clutch to get him into second gear, when he's cold. Oh, and the engine can stall if you don't give it a little extra gas when you pop into fourth."

I stroked the trembling fender in genuine affection. I knew she'd kill the engine when she tried to use the clutch pedal. Then she'd back up to turn around and probably hit something, and I could imagine Horse lurching and heaving up and down when she tried to get back to the highway.

"And you'd better turn on the headlights before you try to drive out of here. Even if Bud and Cliff see you, I'll be over the fence and gone before they can get here. Are you *sure* you can handle a clutch . . . ?"

Hank gave me her sweetest smile, the one that falls somewhere between indulgence and tolerance. It's the smile she usually reserves for truant students. She rolled up the window, gunned Horse's big V8, and left me standing there in the night-cloaked junkyard.

And I mean *left* me there. I had scarcely stepped back out of the way when she revved the engine to a full roar and I heard the big metal *clack* of Horse's long shift lever going into reverse. The headlight beams swept the clearing in a perfect arc as she backed up. Then *my* truck, that faithless illegitimate son of a Plymouth, slid smoothly into second for her and took off up the road like a greyhound—the dog, not the bus—out of the starting gate. "In an instant", as it says in Robert Burns's poem, "all was dark."

Exhaust fumes and fine dust shown in the starlight along the dirt track. I heard Hank make the stop at the highway and saw the headlights swing south when she started up again, the engine revving through three gear changes, and then I was alone in the silence. No wind, no jets in the sky, no sounds from the highway. Just Nebraska, the night, the silence.

My eyes adjusted and I started south, leaving the maze of car bodies hemming in the deep gloom like the walls of a wizard's castle. I stepped over the fence, holding the sagging wire down with my stick, and entered the wheat field.

"Here he goes," I muttered. "D. Lachlan McIntyre following yet another literary hunch. Following the *feeling* again."

Moving in the gloom across the gentle ruts between the standing grain, listening and looking, straining to see whatever lay ahead, I rapidly metamorphosed into a character out of the novel. I was an invisible figure, an omniscient narrator walking beside the two lovers fleeing the English village after the murder.

The wheat field wasn't difficult to negotiate in the dark because the furrows were so evenly spaced and regular I could move in a steady rhythm. Holding my hands and stick out ahead of me, I managed to walk without breaking down the wheat. But at the far edge of the field things were different. The stars gave me enough light to show I was at the end of the wheat, but the moon was in its last quarter and low on the horizon, so all was black before me. Like a blind man I explored the shallow dry ditch with sweeps of my stick. I stepped into it and went up to my knees in Russian thistle and goat-head burrs. The four-strand barbed-wire fence ran along the lip of the ditch, forcing me to get face down in the dirt, nettles, and thistles to wiggle underneath the bottom strand of wire.

In the next field, alfalfa grabbed at my ankles and uneven humps in the ground threatened to send me sprawling.

While I normally don't mind the smell of alfalfa, this stuff was awful, like the smell of cow urine mixed with lavender soap. The dew on it didn't help anything, making the plants slippery as I trod them down. There was irony in it, too; there probably aren't more than a dozen alfalfa fields within ten miles of Alliance, and I had to go straight through one of them.

At the edge of the alfalfa I paused. I was in an unused field of native grass. Jane Eyre would have thrown herself down in the gently whispering verdure, but apparently Jane Eyre—or Brontë—didn't live where they have sandburs, nettles, gnats, mosquitoes, ants, and, best of all, chiggers. Lie down with those and you rise up with a rash.

What would my quarry be thinking at this point? If they got to this point. I hadn't told Hank or Houghton why I thought the two fugitives had walked south from their abandoned car. Logically they should have continued north, the direction they were going when they ran out of gas and decided to hide the car on the deserted farm road. There they had stumbled into the junkyard and had had some hope, for a few minutes, of getting gasoline from one of the junked cars.

I looked south. The sky was beginning to show gray. Dark shadows off to my left showed where a deep arroyo wound among the hills. I could see a windmill tower against the far skyline. It meant water. Water, and possibly people. Would they have walked toward people, or away from them? Would they have stayed in the open fields, or have tried to stay in the shelter of the windbreaks and wooded draws and gullies where they wouldn't have been seen?

It was just barely getting light, and the only people up at this hour would be doing barn chores, milking cattle, fueling up machinery. No one would be out in the fields yet, so Cass and Michael would probably have felt safe staying in the fields a while longer. I crossed a dirt road, which meant scrunching myself under two more fences and struggling through two more ditches. But that early in the morning there was no one on the road. I could see the faint glow of Alliance over the horizon, far off in the distance. Following the fields would have taken them toward it.

After the road, I found myself next to a thick, dark windbreak. There was a row of elms or some kind of deciduous trees, then a row of densely planted pines, then two rows of dense, tall cedars. It was all but impenetrable and made a good deep shadow to hide in. When I came to the end of it and crossed the narrow road leading to a farmhouse, a cornfield offered more concealment. It was clumsy walking, though. The rows ran at right angles to my line of travel, so, instead of just strolling down an aisle between the stalks, I had to squeeze between the plants and step from ridge to ridge. Sharp-edged leaves felt like knives on my hands and face and I was accumulating a shirt full of bugs. As I moved from left to right, I tended to lose my bearings. But when the corn was finally behind me, there was enough pre-dawn light to show me my surroundings. I was at the edge of a hill of native grass and brush sloping toward a river bottom.

The gravity pulling me down the slope gave me a feeling of euphoria, the sensation of doing a telemark on cross-country skis, the same feeling of weightlessness meeting smooth resistance. Down I strode, high grass whishing against my legs. I could see for miles in the pre-dawn light and felt I could go loping down such hills forever. Sometimes I would have to scramble up out of a sandy cattle trail, sometimes I had to use my hands to heave myself up out of an arroyo, but then I would go striding along again, caught up in the pleasure of movement.

I imagined Cass and Michael having done the same thing, coming to the hill and running down it, suddenly breathless and clinging deliriously to each other, laughing as the tension momentarily let go its hold.

Pausing for breath and a drink, I saw a train on the distant horizon, just a little black streak crawling along the crest of the world. Would Cass and Michael have seen a train on those tracks? Would they have thought about trying to jump a freight to get away? No. It didn't seem right for her character. From what I knew of Cass Deering, she was a woman who needed to know where she was headed, and why. She would not be taken to destinations not of her choosing.

The terrain flattened into marshy meadowland concealing narrow ribbons of flowing water and soggy stretches where the ground shivered like gelatin as I stepped on it. I came to a halt at the edge of a slow stream. The Niobrara.

Although I was sure I could jump over it, or at least wade it, I walked a ways downstream to look for a bridge. Nothing. But turning and walking upstream quite a distance, I saw the highway bridge. It was a long one, spanning not only the little stream but the valley the stream ran through. It was a good twenty feet above the stream bottom; a person walking across it would be running a risk of being seen by passing cars. Something about it *felt* funny, but I decided to ignore it. Cass and Michael would have arrived here in daylight, and wouldn't have taken a chance on it.

I walked back downstream, letting the *feeling* probe the terrain and bushes, and a half mile or more from the highway I came to where a midstream sandbar offered a way to cross over. The *feeling* was strong there. The water was deep along the edges, but I could jump to the sand, and then to the other bank. While I was standing there, debating whether the sandbar was solid or squishy, the edge of the fierce yellow sun poked up over the hill and threw morning beams of light into the thickets on the opposite shore.

Suddenly a dark cave-like shadow emerged in the slanting light, some kind of crude shelter in the willows. Tired and hungry with daylight coming, perhaps my fugitives had decided they would cross the stream, and then hide in the brush to rest. I was willing to bet that they had also considered using the highway bridge—which would account for the strange twitch of the *feeling* it gave me—and then they had walked downstream to where no one would see them. The *feeling* told me they had crossed here, so here I would cross as well.

You never know for sure how deep a stream is going to be, as I've learned from fly-fishing. But as I've also learned, you generally find out.

The Niobrara illustrates a rule of hydraulics involving speed and volume. When water flowing through alluvial soil encounters a rising riverbed, such as a sandbar, the same volume of water must pass through a reduced channel. Therefore it either accelerates or it digs a deeper channel.

In this case, it did both. Standing on the grassy bank and probing for the bottom with one foot, I lost my balance and tumbled in. I had planned on getting my feet wet, but, now that I was on my knees, the Niobrara was filling my shoes and my pockets. I stumbled to my feet and clumsily waded toward midstream, hoping the water wouldn't get any deeper. Palmer would love this, I thought. She'd probably whip out her camera and take a picture to post on the faculty web page.

On the other side, I clawed at the grass and scrubby willows to get ashore. Dripping, cussing, and shivering, I was almost over the feeling I was enjoying myself.

My first impulse was to look for shelter from the open air. My back and legs were starting to feel sore and my stomach was rumbling at me. What I wanted was somewhere to curl up and rest and dry out. Cass and Michael would have felt the same way, and right there, where I had come ashore, was the crude bower of willows, just the right size for a person to huddle in.

It wasn't a natural bower. Although it was pretty obvious animals had used it, no animal had built it. And it wasn't new. Somebody had bent willows over into an arch, twisting the branches together to make a crude shelter. The broken branches were dried out and the bark was cracked open. The green branches twisted into each other and had new shoots and leaves on them.

So, I reasoned, sitting there, shivering, some kid could have made this, or some bum caught in a rainstorm. But, I argued to myself, it could have been Cass and Michael. I wanted it to have been them. The *feeling* told me I was right.

Warmed a little, I got up and moved on. Within twenty or thirty yards, I stepped out of the willows and onto a well-used narrow dirt road that probably led to a farm.

What would Cass and Michael have done here? On the other side of the road were a tight fence, a thickly grown windbreak of trees and thorny-looking bushes, and a very big open field beyond. Westward, the road would take them to the highway where they might be discovered. The logical thing to have done would have been to walk eastward to see if they could have found the end of the field or another road going south. Maybe an abandoned farm.

I walked into the morning sun, letting its heat and the

movement of my arms and legs warm me up. I was still wet when I came in sight of the house, but I was no longer chilled. At least I wasn't chilled until I felt something hard and round pressed against my spine.

"Hands up, mister," said the voice behind me.

I complied.

"Whatta ya want here?" the voice said.

Very slowly, very gingerly, keeping my hands in the air, I carefully turned around to face my assailant. He was a kid of about ten years, holding a single-shot .22 on me.

"Good morning." I smiled.

The kid just kept looking at me with that dead-pan expression kids wear when they are sizing you up.

"Nice gun," I went on, still smiling. "It's a Stevens, isn't it? Friend of mine had one when I was a kid. I had an old Remington pump, myself. But it only shot Twenty-Two shorts." I shook my head in self-sympathy for a little boy whose parents wouldn't buy him a better rifle than that.

The boy took a half step backward when I looked at his rifle, but still held his ground with that dead-pan glare on his face.

"I'm on a kind of survey," I told him, "walking across the sand hills." I attempted an ingratiating chuckle and looked down at my wet clothes. "I fell into the river back there!" The kid apparently didn't find it amusing. "Are your folks around?" I asked.

He was still eyeing me suspiciously, but eventually he decided I was harmless and lowered the muzzle of the .22. "C'mon," he said. He led me toward the house, giving me an armed escort through a pack of three dogs. Leaving the dogs to guard me, he vanished inside.

My only option appeared to be to remain as motionless as possible. Within a few minutes, to my great relief, the lady of the house appeared on the front porch and ordered the dogs to lie down. Or, to be more accurate, to "lay" down.

"They'll bark, but they don't bother anybody. They'd be licking your hand in another minute. Won't you come on in?"

Hospitality is a point of pride with sand hills people, and this woman was no exception. She ushered me down a cool dim hallway into the kitchen, where she motioned for me to take a chair at the kitchen table. She asked if I'd like a cup of coffee and a cinnamon roll. "Kind of stale," she apologized. "I made them yesterday."

She insisted on putting my boots and socks into the clothes dryer for a few minutes, so there I sat barefoot in a warm kitchen, sipping excellent coffee and sinking my teeth into a home-made roll. It may have been yesterday's pastry, with just a very slight crispiness to the outer crust, but it was wonderful. It was sticky with sugar and cinnamon and slathered with real butter. While my hostess busied herself with the clothes dryer in the adjoining room, I debated the idea of editing a cookbook collection of pastry recipes. Imagine doing this kind of research all summer!

"To tell the truth," I said above the rumble of the dryer, "I'm sort of following the trail of a young lady, maybe a young lady and her boyfriend, who might have come through here last summer. The girl in the murder case?"

She knew the case, and knew that the girl, or the murderer, had not been found.

"Well," she said, coming to refill my coffee cup, "we didn't see anybody around here."

"Oh," I said. "I guess they might have passed you by. It just seemed logical, after crossing the Niobrara down there, that they might have been ready to stop hiding and walk to a farmhouse to get some food and get warm."

"Well . . . there was the missing food," she said.

"Missing food?"

"Oh, yes. We were in town . . . no, that's not right. This was the time we went to visit Frank's folks for three days. Anyway, around here we never lock our doors, and, after we got back, I went to get a can of beans from the cupboard and it wasn't there. And there was a loaf of bread missing from the freezer . . . I make my own bread and freeze it, it keeps better that way. Oh, and several jars of preserves. Let me think. Yes, some of my canned Niagra grapes were missing . . . and pickled beets and a couple of jars of sauerkraut. Oh, and apricots. We have an old tree that's always loaded with them. Almost break the branches down. I think there were some cans of sardines gone . . . I don't like the darn' things, but Frank does. We thought somebody must have come in while we were gone and helped themselves. Well, we *know* somebody did. There was even a grain sack gone that I kept out on the porch to gather potatoes and onions with. I didn't miss it until later." She paused to top off my coffee.

"John, that's our boy, you know, he took the dogs and they found a scent trail leading right on south, right across the fence and out over the potato field. Strange direction to go. It's really hard walking out there. Oh, and speaking of strange! We think they took a blanket off the line out there."

"Strange?" I said.

"It was an electric blanket. Kind of old, but it still worked. I had washed it and hung it out to dry before we left, and I guess whoever it was took the food also took that blanket. But it wouldn't work without the control and the cord. Strange."

156

"Still, it was a blanket," I said, setting the cup down. "A person sleeping out in the open would be pretty tempted to steal it."

The boy and his three-dog pack were only too happy to show me where they found the scent trail last summer. When his mother had found things missing, he had set out with his dogs and his gun to find the bad guy, and he wasn't scared, either. As he talked, he led me south across a wide fallow field until we came to a tightly strung barbed-wire fence marking the edge of the farm. He said proudly that his dogs followed the scent "in a beeline, by golly" right to this place. He even found where somebody had ripped their shirt climbing under the fence. There'd been a scrap of cloth, hanging right there. By golly.

In that country it's bad manners to climb on a tightly strung fence or to push the wire down to get across. So I tossed my pack over and followed it by getting down on my belly and scooching under the bottom strand. Standing up and brushing myself off, I took up my pack to continue my walk.

"Thanks for the help," I said to the boy.

"No problem," he replied.

"Oh," I added, "by the way! Do you know anything about a sort of shelter over there on the river? Kind of a little cave somebody made in the willows?"

"Sure."

It figured. When I was a boy of John's size, I knew every stick, rock, and unlocked building for five miles around.

"I seen it 'long about the same time we missed the food," the boy explained. "I told my dad about it, and he thought maybe some bum stopped there an' camped."

"That's probably it," I said. "Well, so long. Thanks for the help."

"No problem."

It was with a sad, nostalgic smile that I watched him skipping home with his dogs. It reminded me of the days before I fell into literature, those boy days of mine, filled with important adventure. All summer I went abroad in the meadow and along the stream, threatening varmints and imaginary villains with my empty gun, monitoring the shape and movement of mountain clouds, supervising the dog, and guarding all the approaches to our place while my mother worked in the kitchen or the garden.

The sun now bore down on the wheat like it was trying to roast it right there in the field, and me along with it. I crossed wheat fields and quarter-sections of wild grass standing nearly chest high, detoured around sudden drop-offs into arroyos, and came to what looked like a whole section populated by cattle. A bull stood sentinel over the cows, looking like a locomotive mounted on four legs. I briefly considered what the odds were that I could outrun him, and ended up deciding to detour around this particular field.

Another creek crossing gave my boots and pant legs a second soaking, and the water helped the burrs and dust adhere better. And don't let anyone tell you Nebraska is flat and dry. Long rolling slopes took me up and down, down and up, around hills and through gullies where stagnant water blossomed with green duckweed and long-tendrilled slime.

Reaching another road, I had another decision for the *feeling* to make. Which way would my two fictional characters have gone? Had they known the terrain better now that they were closer to Alliance?

I found a stump in the shade of a cottonwood, and it looked relatively free of ticks, ants, spiders, and stickers, so I sat down on it to rest and think. It wasn't long before the thinking led to a puzzling thought, either. Why Alliance? If I was right and the pair had come this way, and if they had headed for Alliance . . . *why?* Why return there?

One reason might have been that they had nowhere else to go. After a couple of days on foot, they may have realized that they could either stay out of sight and starve, or they could get to a road and, sooner or later, get picked up. Chances were that anyone seeing them on a road would have called the sheriff or the state patrol.

Then again . . . they had taken an awful chance, stealing food and a blanket from a farmhouse. If all they had wanted was to get to Alliance and turn themselves in to Bob Houghton, who Cass would trust, why not just have gotten to the highway to find a ride into town? What else were they doing out here in the countryside?

So far, I felt that they had always traveled south and east. So I reluctantly left my shady stump and resumed my hike, going along the road into the sun. The hill I was on seemed to have no end to it, but eventually I topped the rise and saw that the road ended at a sand hill shimmering away out there in the distance, with no shelter in sight, not a house or a barn or a shed. If—when—Michael and Cass had stood here, they would have also been feeling the heat, provided that the day was clear and sunny like this one, but they would have not been in a panic. The initial shock and fear would have dissipated and they would have been trying to reason out what to do. They had had food and a blanket. What else did they need? Shelter. Some kind of hide-out. Some place to hole up until dark.

I turned around and backtracked myself westward,

passing the place where I had come out of the fields onto the road. The sun was now cooking the earth, as if sucking the air away from the ground and leaving me only the heat to breathe. Many a Nebraska native would say it was just a pleasantly warm summer day, but to a Greenie from the Colorado foothills, it felt like Satan's own sauna. My neck and my arms seemed to be glowing. I wanted to strip off my shirt even though the sun would broil me like a cheap piece of flank steak. Heat waves rose in snaky ranks all around me. Nothing moved along the weed-filled ditches and under the weedy fence lines. Except for some motionless cattle under the shade of a lone cottonwood, I seemed to be the only breathing, living thing in all that country. What wouldn't I give to be inside a house with air conditioning?

Inside a house. Damn! Between paying attention to the sandburs and sunburn, not to mention being preoccupied with the heat, I had forgotten to keep thinking like Cass. Sure, this was a hot, dry, Nebraska countryside, not a damp, cold, depressing English midlands heath. That didn't matter. That novel was drawing her onward, guiding her steps as if she were the heroine herself. Inside a house, I realized. Inside a house. Cass had known all these roads around here, she knew the terrain and the farms and the roads. She wasn't lost.

She knew where she had been going, she and Michael with their food and blanket. And now I knew, too, except that it would take me longer to discover the right place. I took a deep drink of water and went on walking.

After an hour that seemed more like four, I spotted a rectangular road marker on a steel post, weaving and wobbling in the heat like a dancing mirage. When I trudged up to it, it said: **Cty A7**.

It was at the very next rising of County Alternate 7 that

the *feeling* really kicked in. Right ahead of me, where shimmering waves of heat made the prairie look like an old daguerreotype under warped glass, was the house. I almost didn't want it to be there, but there it was. Cass had known it was there.

It sat a quarter mile back from the road, isolated and desolated, but even at that distance it was obvious the place was deserted. I walked on until I came to the turn-off leading from the county road to the ancient two-story relic. I treated myself to another long drink of water, then took out my cell phone. While Hank's phone was ringing, I closed my eyes and tested the gut *feeling* one more time. This felt right. This was it.

"Hank?" I said. "It's me. I found the house I wanted. Yep, I'm pretty sure this is it. Can you come on out and get me? Great. Should take you maybe half an hour, forty-five minutes. I'm not sure how far I am from the highway. Just head north on Three Fifty-Seven to where the junction is, and right around there somewhere you should find a dirt road marked County A-Seven. It probably goes east from the junction, and pretty soon it has to take a turn to the north. Where I'm standing it runs north and south. OK? Great. See you soon. Look for a big two-story abandoned house on the south side of the road. 'Bye."

I walked on down the lane to the house, where I sat in its shade to gulp down more water. I took out a power bar and ate it in spite of the fact that the heat of my backpack had melted it into something that seemed like peanut-butter-flavored wood putty. The backpack, one of my old favorites, was faded, stained, and torn in places; my hiking pants were ripped across one knee and smeared with mud, and my good old khaki shirt showed large underarm blotches of salt-rimmed sweat. All in all, the derelict house and the

derelict professor sitting in the shade made a matched set. Anyone coming along would take me for a tramp, I thought. But who would come along this forlorn stretch of road?

No Henriette Palmer, not yet, so I got up, stretched, and decided to take a look around. The house looked as if it had four rooms upstairs, and each room had two narrow windows, those old-fashioned double hung windows whose sills come down almost to the floor. They were boarded up from within. The roof shingles were faded to gray and some were missing, but it still could be weather tight. Two things made this old farmhouse seem especially sad. First, the Nebraska sun and wind long ago had stripped it of paint and left it looking naked, warped, and forgotten. Second, the front porch supports had rotted and fallen, letting the shingled roof sag precipitously. Where children, their parents, guests, and strangers had once mounted the wide steps into the shade of the broad inviting porch to arrive at the front door with its big window and elaborate molding, now it was necessary to crouch under the edge of the fallen roof. The porch floor was rotten, broken in places. A sheet of peeling plywood was nailed over the front entrance.

Around back, I noticed that newer boards had been nailed over the kitchen door. In the yard, there was an outhouse leaning windward and a collapsed equipment shed, or maybe it had been a shed for the family car. Anyway, it had leaned leeward until it had fallen over altogether. Would there have been indoor plumbing? I wondered. I went toward the back of what used to be the yard and was now a dusty expanse of weeds until I could see the roof. Yes, plumbing. I could see the vent pipes sticking up, one over the kitchen, and one where the bathroom must be.

Near where I was standing there was a rusty oil drum,

the kind some people use for incinerators. In it, under moldy cardboard, an old license plate, a rotted throw rug, and two broken whiskey bottles, I found a black plastic garbage bag. It was a little brittle but still intact. Gingerly undoing the faded twist tie, I opened it up and found a discarded blanket. A pale green electric blanket.

Carrying the garbage bag back to the shade of the house, I dragged the blanket out. It had been wrapped around two sardine tins, four Mason jars, three bean cans that looked as if they had been opened with a chisel, and a pop bottle. Judging from the evidence, I had to think that somebody had gathered up the refuse, put it on the blanket, put the blanket into a trash bag along with some old newspapers and junk, and then dropped the bag into the backyard oil drum.

The crunch of tires on gravel announced Professor Palmer's arrival. The absence of roar and racket meant she had brought her Buick, instead of Horse. That was good; the air conditioning would feel wonderful.

I came around the corner of the house, toting the garbage bag over my shoulder and my grimy backpack in my other hand. Standing beside her car, Hank took one look at me and went into gales of laughter. Well, maybe not gales, but she laughed. She laughed—how can I say it?—freely and without the slightest sign of good manners.

"Excuse me!" she called out as if she didn't recognize me. "I was looking for a Professor McIntyre! Have you seen him? You poor man! You look hungry and homeless! Perhaps I can let you have a dollar for a meal!"

"Funny," I said.

"No, seriously!" she went on gleefully, probably wishing she had her camera, "I think the Salvation Army will take you in, once they see you."

She slid back into the car to get out of the heat and popped the trunk so I could put the bag and my pack in it. I opened the passenger's side and flopped down gratefully in the chilled air. I looked down at my stained and ripped pants, and caught a whiff of my own body odor. Nice study in contrasts, I thought, seeing how clean and cool Hank looked. Seeing how clean and cool she looked, in fact, made me feel filthy, hot, and unbearable.

As Hank's long tan leg put the pedal to the Buick and we tore back down the dirt road, I realized the importance of what I had just been thinking. Like Professor Palmer, Cass Deering was a woman who was careful of her appearance. If she had made the walk that I just made, she would be looking almost as bad and feeling as dirty and sweaty as I did. And if she had stayed at this house, as I suspected she did, and then had walked the next fifteen or twenty miles toward Alliance, she would have looked awful, and she would have taken pains to avoid people. The heroine in the novel went through the same feelings.

The parallel was holding. So where, I wondered, was the next stop?

"Why so quiet?" Hank asked, looking over at me—and wrinkling her nose.

"Thinking about that house back there," I said. "I'm going back tomorrow and check it out, maybe find the owner. I think Michael and Cass left the stuff in that plastic bag there, and I think the owner threw it out. Maybe Bob Houghton can find some fingerprints on the bottles and cans. Let's drop them off at the police station, then I'll get cleaned up and buy you supper . . . how about that?"

"You don't look like you could buy supper for yourself, let alone me!" She laughed. "Anyway, do you want me to go with you tomorrow?"

"You need to get to Lincoln," I reminded her. "The interview about your manuscript?"

"It can wait. I'll phone them. Now that I've seen the house, I think I know what you're up to, and I'm curious. It's the Hardy novel, right?"

"You've read it?"

"Not that I remember. But I saw the movie on TV."

"Great," I said. "Just like my students. Saw the film, read the Cliff Notes, and you're ready for the exam."

"All I *said* was that I wouldn't mind coming along to watch you work this one out . . . if you do. So?"

I looked over at her, sitting behind the wheel with her head up and her chin forward, the very picture of poise. Did she really want to watch the McIntyre mind as it went about brilliantly solving another puzzle, or did she just enjoy watching me crash and burn? I leaned back and closed my eyes and let the air conditioning blow chilled air over me.

"So, OK," I said.

Chapter Eleven

She only said, "The night is dreary,
He cometh not," she said;
She said, "I am aweary, aweary,
I would that I were dead!"
"Mariana"
—Alfred Lord Tennyson

He was going to come. She was sure of it!
Madame Bovary
—Gustave Flaubert

I phoned home that evening to tell Aggie I'd be another few days in Nebraska. "I'm not sure I can say how things will work out here," I said. While I talked, I was pushing note cards and photographs around on the trailer's dinette table, organizing them by subject. "But I'll be home by next Monday, in any case," I went on. "Tuesday's the day we need to leave for New Mexico, right? For the opening of that exhibit at the Museum of Indian Arts?"

"Oh, David! I forgot you wanted to go to Albuquerque! Oh, I am so sorry!"

"Problem?" I asked.

"The provost asked me to sit in for him at the first concert of the symphony season. He can't make it, so I said I'd do it."

"The symphony's opening day, huh? Do you get to throw out the first cellist?" I said.

"Silly. No. But there's more. The symphony board was looking for a place for the guest conductor and his wife to stay, and I said we'd love to have them as our house guests. Just for two nights. The dean of liberal arts is throwing a cocktail party after the concert."

"Well," I said gallantly, "I'll try to get things wrapped up here and come on home for that. What night is it?"

"Oh, well . . . ," she hesitated.

"Problem?" I said. Again.

"Please don't . . . well, don't think you *need* to be here. Not on my account. I can handle things just fine. You need to stay and finish your project, or whatever. Did you find the missing girl, by the way? And her friend . . . what was his name . . . Michael?"

"Haven't found them," I said, "but I found her trail and I think I know where she is. No idea where he went. I think they were headed for Alliance, but something happened to them. I told you my theory that she was acting out the heroine's rôle in that novel. But something messed that up. Somewhere along the way, they got into trouble. Tomorrow morning I'm going to do some more walking and see if our friend Hardy can shed some light on it."

"Marlene and I were chatting the other day, and I told her about this mystery you've gotten yourself into. We had quite a good time, thinking up various plots. Do you want to hear one?"

"Sure, go ahead," I said.

"We were thinking . . . it was actually my idea . . . that this girl who vanished has gone to live with her sister. You said her sister was a dancer in another town."

"That's right."

"Well, what if . . . just what if, you understand . . . what if she was living with this sister and they look so much alike that they can actually fool people into thinking they are just *one* person! Wouldn't that be fun? It would be an ideal way to hide. Just convince the police that every time they get a report of this one girl living in that town, it's really her sister. Then the real one could go out, dressed like her sister, and go shopping, even get a job, and nobody would know."

"I'll think about it," I said. "Anyway, I'll try to get home by next Sunday. Or I'll call you if my plans change."

"That's nice," she said absently. Then she quickly added: "But I don't want you to rush yourself. I'm awfully busy here, and everything is fine. I'll block out some time later in the month for us to go to Albuquerque and see the exhibit."

I put the phone away and drank my coffee. Sometimes it was amazing how well Aggie and I understood each other. I understood she would feel more comfortable at the concert gala without my smirky-face presence. She'd be free to schmooze around the cocktail party and even go out for drinks afterward if someone suggested it. And she understood I would rather trudge through creeks and poison ivy than play house host to some *prima donna* conductor and his wife.

The photograph in front of me was the one of Cass Deering and her sister and father standing by their shiny new station wagon, one of those long, heavy, box-shaped models with phony air scoops aft of the side windows and phony wood grain panels trimmed in wide printed wood strips decorated with big phony chrome carriage bolt heads. It contrasted with the genuine smiles and obvious affection shared by the three people in the picture, a caring father and two down-to-earth genuine girls.

Actually, even with all its decorative features, it was a

nice-looking car. It had nice proportions and a kind of streamlined style. What did Ronnie Webber say it was? An Estate Wagon? No, that's not right. I looked at my note on the back of the picture. Country Squire. It didn't matter. I filled two water bottles and put them in my pack along with a couple of apples and energy bars, checked the first aid emergency equipment, and hung the pack on the doorknob. At dawn the search would be on again.

Punctual Professor Palmer pulled up to the trailer before sunrise. It's a funny thing: she loves getting up early in the morning, loves to get out and jog or bike as the sun is coming up, yet she has no interest in backpack camping. I love crawling out of a tent at sunrise, surrounded by all the new sights and sounds of a fresh day, but Hank wouldn't sleep outside if you held a pistol to her head.

Anyway, she showed up in time to catch me brushing my teeth. I filled my thermal mug with the remainder of the breakfast coffee, grabbed my backpack, and, ten minutes later, she was driving us north through the untouched quiet of the pre-dawn world. From my window, I watched the faint glow over the eastern horizon turning to a light bluish band between an umber earth and iron-colored sky. I watched the dark tips of the power poles whip by and sipped my coffee and relaxed to the sensation of the empty road and the sleeping landscape waiting out there in the dim early light, waiting for another blistering hot day to begin.

"Lachlan," Hank said.

"Yes?" I answered.

"I thought of something last night," she said, eyes on the road.

"So did I, but I'm married."

"You're a married Cretin," she snapped.

"What is it?"

"This theory about Cass following the plot of a novel, just because it's about a woman in sort of the same circumstance," she said.

"What about it?"

"I tried to remember how the novel ends. It seems to me you're limiting your information base. As scientific method, it's inadequate."

"Thank you very much, Professor. What's inadequate about it?"

"Did you ever stop to think that she could be following a book. . . ."

"That *is* the idea," I interrupted.

". . . but that it's a book other than one with a woman's name for a title? It doesn't necessarily have to be one from the list you gave her. Maybe it's *Of Mice and Men* or *Little House on the Prairie* or something."

"Thanks, Palmer," I said. "That really opens things up."

Hank was right. I had a sudden flashback to those undergraduate literature classes where professors forced us to ferret out the sources and derivations of every literary work ever written. What were the sources of Tennyson's "Idylls of the King"? What did Hemingway read about Africa? What else did Cass Deering read?

I would have made a devastating retort, but the deserted house came into view.

We left the car and walked around, looking for a way to get inside. To be honest, I was the only one doing the snooping. I ducked under the sagging porch roof and tried to wiggle the plywood nailed over the door, then I went around the house testing the boards covering the windows.

I even tried to open the cellar door, but it was securely bolted from the inside.

Palmer hung back, nervously watching the road like we were breaking into a bank and she was the look-out. I don't know whether it's because she's honest and respectful of other people's property or just one of the scary nervous sort, but she never was very good at trespassing, not to mention breaking and entering.

I was sort of accidentally pulling on one of the boards nailed over the kitchen door—just making sure it was secure, you know—when Palmer made her second disturbing remark of the morning.

"Oops!"

"Oops?"

I turned to see what her problem was. Here it came, a squat little Fordson tractor, the silhouette unmistakable even in dawn light, painted battleship gray with a single headlight like a Cyclops' eye. It came puttering at top speed straight toward us out of the sunrise.

Let's see, I thought. If I remember my college physics, the formula is something like F=ma. Force equals mass times acceleration. That little gray tractor probably weighs as much as a small car, let's say a ton and a half. OK, that's the mass. The acceleration is probably fifteen miles per hour, which means it will hit us with a force of . . . ?

"She looks serious," said Hank.

I looked. The squat little tractor was driven by an equally squat little woman wearing a determined look on her face and holding a large shotgun upright with one hand while she steered the bouncing tractor with the other. OK, I thought, forget F=ma and start thinking muzzle velocity of a 12-gauge Remington.

She brought the tractor to such an abrupt stop that it

stalled the engine and an ominous silence came rolling back over the plains. I heard a far-off meadowlark announcing his territory from atop a fence post and wondered if it would be the last bird I would ever hear.

The woman dismounted without taking her fierce little eyes off of us, and she brought her shotgun with her.

"Back again, are ya?" she yelled. "Some people got no damn' respect for other people's property! This time I'm takin' your names and gettin' the license number of that car and I'm phonin' the sheriff. Sick *and* tired of bums and kids usin' this place for a flop."

Hank sheltered herself behind me. "Think you can get us out of this?" she whispered into my ear.

"Ma'am," I began, "maybe you can help us. . . ."

"Help you to a jail cell, that's what! What're you two doin' this time, figurin' to find some antiques to steal? You're sure as hell too old t'be lookin' for a place to neck in."

"Better let that one go," Hank whispered from behind me.

"No, we wouldn't steal anything. I've got a card from the police sergeant, here, in my shirt pocket . . ."—but I *didn't* have Houghton's calling card. That shirt was in the trailer in the laundry box.

"Maybe you should look around for a stick," Hank whispered.

"Now, ma'am . . ."—I smiled at the little lady with the big gun—"if I can just explain what we're doing. . . ."

Hank stepped out from behind me. She had noticed how carefully the woman was keeping the shotgun muzzle pointed skyward. Palmer always could read character better than I could.

"If you don't mind," Hank began, "if I could just ask . . .

have you lived around here very long?"

"All my life," snapped the woman. "Right over that hill. And you're trespassing on my property." But her eyes showed a curious softening. Maybe the adrenaline of her tractor ride was wearing off.

"Then we were wondering . . . that is . . . my colleague and I really do have the blessings of the Alliance police department. We're working on an idea about that poor girl who disappeared a year ago. Cass Deering."

"Heard of it," the woman said. "What do you two have to do with it?"

Hank was drawing on the inborn lust for gossip, and it seemed to be working.

"Our idea is . . . and Bob Houghton agrees . . . that maybe they came through here, on foot. They might have used this house for refuge. Did you happen to see anything suspicious last year?"

"Hah!" the tractor lady snorted. "Did I? Did I? You darn' right I did. Paid a man good money to put three-quarter inch plywood on those windows and make me a plywood shutter with a hasp for that door there, and it's no sooner done than somebody decides it's a free hotel and broke in anyway. Busted the hasp an' tore the plywood off a upstairs window."

"Did you see them? Did they have a car?"

"No. Saw the mess, though. I figure they were here three, four days. They left a blanket on one of the old mattresses, all stained with love juice, if you know what I mean, and they left dirty cans and bottles . . . good way t'attract rats . . . and burned a couple of my kitchen chairs in the stove. I just wish I'd seen the smoke, dang 'em. I'd've come and give 'em a hot time, all right. Do you know, they used the toilet even though the water's shut off. Darn' mess."

"And I guess you were the one who had to clean it all up," I commiserated, hoping she'd mention the trash barrel without my having to admit to robbing it the day before.

"Who else? I hauled four buckets of water upstairs to flush out that toilet. An' the rest of the junk I bagged up and tossed inta that barrel there. You can look at it if you want."

"OK," I said. "But you didn't see them."

"Saw one, I think. The man."

"You know it was a man and a woman? How?"

The tractor lady gave Hank an odd look, and then both of them looked at me the same way.

"The shape that blanket was in, I don't think it was two men."

"Oh."

"Anyways," the tractor lady continued, "I found the busted door hasp, and then found that mess on . . . let's see, I guess it was a Monday. Nope, I'm wrong. Tuesday. It was Tuesday, 'cause my egg buyer comes on Tuesdays and I was complainin' to him about it. But they were gone by then, see. But th' next day after that, I was up there on th' hill and seen a man walkin' north along the road. Can't say why, but I just kinda knew it was one of them. Maybe 'cause we don't get so many people walkin' around out in this country. Anyway, good riddance to 'em, I say."

"North?"

Yes, north. Damn. Assuming this was Michael, why did he go north?

The tractor lady finally grudgingly believed us when we said that we were looking for clues to Cass's disappearance. She gave me permission to walk south across her land.

"Nuthin' but thistles and barbed wire and snakes out there," she said. She said she would telephone her neighbor on the next section and tell him I was going to cross his place as well. The sun was climbing and the day was already warming up when I got my stick and pack from the car, smeared sunscreen on my neck and arms, and started south. Turning to look back, I saw Hank and the tractor lady standing there by the Fordson, chatting away like two long-time friends. They were looking in my direction, and I could have sworn that the shorter of the two had her index finger to her head the way people do when they are talking about some other person's sanity. Or lack of it.

The meadowlark whistled his off-pitch rendition of the "Caprice" from Bernstein's *Candide*, practicing those same six or seven notes over and over again by way of inviting the rest of the world to come see the wonderful fence post he had found. A cock pheasant broke cover to dash ahead of me down the furrows of a long-since abandoned alfalfa field. With the baroque pattern etched on his golden feathers and the thick red rouge on his cheeks, he looked Oriental and out of place. He belonged in an Asian garden of immaculate lawn and sculpted hedges, not here in the dust and thistles.

Clouds came up as I made my way southward, high fluffy ones. Their bottoms flattened as if sitting on an invisible crystal dome, the tops heaped and piled like cauliflower heads. They began to drift into dense masses, and I felt a breeze begin to tickle the hair on my arms.

I came to an old one-room schoolhouse surrounded by a field of last year's straw roughly plowed. One window looked open, and it was. The others had heavy metal screens fastened on with lag screws. There was nothing inside except for dust and some old grain sacks and a square of bricks in the center of the floor where the stove once stood. Out back, there was a pump and an outhouse on the verge of collapse. I couldn't get the pump to work. Maybe my two literary fugitives had come this way, but they hadn't stopped here—except to try the pump, as I had.

By noon the fat cauliflower clouds had piled up on the western rim of the world like tumbleweeds stacked against a fence. The air was hot despite the steady breeze bending the grass and kicking up miniature tornadoes of dust and weeds. The sun didn't seem to have moved since climbing to the top of the sky overhead; it seemed to be trying to beat down on my head hard enough to drive me into the ground.

My two characters, fugitives, whatever, would have been suffering as I was by now. There was no way I was going to force myself to walk through the heat of that Nebraska afternoon, and there was no way they did it, either. Still taking whatever line of march seemed natural—down into gullies, up along fence lines, avoiding skylines—I found myself not so much trying to get anywhere as trying to find shelter, some place to rest. The walking wasn't bad, but the sun! The sun had me panting like a dog, and, if pigs really do sweat, I was sweating like one.

The hot wind blew dust into my eyes. When I got it cleaned out, I saw another building ahead. It was no doubt as dilapidated, dusty, and inhospitable as the schoolhouse, but it still offered some shade. I trudged toward it, trying to visualize two people a year ago walking the same way, trying to ignore Hank Palmer's suggestion that my book theory could be away off and trying not to think about the tractor lady's notion of having seen Michael walking north, rather than south. North. Why the heck would he be retracing their steps north, and alone?

It had been decades since the house had seen any inhabitants other than skunks and rattlesnakes. It was a very small house of three or four rooms, with an attached shed. My guess was that the north wind had finally blown down the north and east walls, then the roof fell in on the rubble. The south wall was more or less intact, and the roof of the attached shed was still in place—but only because it was resting on a 1940s pickup truck.

For a few minutes I couldn't figure out what seemed odd about this place. Something seemed peculiar—out of place, but not obviously out of place. Then I realized what it was. County A7 ran past it, but in the wrong direction. I walked down the ruts that once were the driveway and checked to make sure it was the county road. It was, and it went east and west, not north and south. With the sun almost directly overhead, it was hard to tell for sure which way was north, so I dug around in my pack for my compass. I was right. The road went the wrong way. There was probably a dogleg in it somewhere ahead of me.

I looked at my watch. It was 1:30 p.m. and close to a 100° out here. I took out the cell phone and called Hank.

"Had enough, have you?" she said merrily.

"I think so," I admitted. "Besides, there's a whopper of a storm making up. What are you up to right now?"

"I'm at the Hut," Hank said, "having iced coffee with Betty and Bob. Sound good?"

"Very good," I said. Ordinarily I would give her a hard time about sitting on her duff in the air conditioning while I was out here suffering, but I was too hot and too tired for it.

"Listen," Hank said, "Bob wants to talk to you. Hold on a second, will you?"

There was a moment of distant voices and shuffling noises, and then Sergeant Houghton was on the line.

"What's up?" I said.

"Got some news for you," the sergeant said. "Found Michael Whyte."

"No kidding!" I said. "Where?"

"Chadron. He died there, a little over a year ago. A trucker had taken him to the emergency room there. He had an accident on Highway Eighty-Seven."

"By the junkyard?" I said. "The one those two old hermits own?"

"No. He hadn't got that far. It was a really freak accident, Doc. This trucker came to the bridge over the Niobrara. You know . . . that big long bridge? He saw a guy sitting on the railing, just staring down into the creek. Another eighteen-wheeler was coming the other way, and they passed each other on the bridge. The driver looked in his mirror just in time to see this guy fall off the railing."

"Holy cow!" I said.

"Yeah. So the driver stopped and went back. The blast of the trucks going by had blown him right off the bridge. Fell about twenty feet. The guy managed to tell the trucker he needed to go for help, or had to get help for somebody, or something like that. But that's all he said."

"So this truck driver took him to Chadron?"

"Yeah. He got him to the emergency ward and that's where he died. Exposure, dehydration, shock. The medical report from the hospital also said he had some really bad intestinal bugs."

"So did you talk to this truck driver?"

"No way. A year ago? No, I got the police report from Chadron."

"How'd you know it was Michael Whyte?"

"Long story. Listen, I'm off duty. Why don't I drive out there and get you. I can fill you in on the way home.

Henriette says you're out there off Highway Eighty-Seven, somewhere."

"Sure," I said, "that's great. Maybe you'd know where I was if I described it?"

"Go ahead."

"I'm at a fallen-down house. A small one. There's an attached shed with an old pickup in it. There's a wide gravel road . . . I think it's A-Seven, before it turns north. It runs east and west in front of this place. I don't suppose you could bring along a beer or two?"

"Might could do that. I think I know the place you mean. If you look, let's see . . . west, I guess . . . can you see a deep draw with a creek in it?"

"Uh, maybe. I see a line of trees, anyway. Probably a creek."

"Yeah, I know where you are. Right south of you, maybe a couple of miles, is where those boys found the charm bracelet. Well, tell you what, Professor, I'll stop off and grab six of ol' Bud's best brew and come look for you."

"Thanks, Bob."

This was a good turn of events. Houghton and I could maybe work out some of the problems with my theory. Meanwhile, I might as well look around.

I stooped and peered under the sloping shed roof. A person could squeeze in here. It was still hot, but, at least, it was out of the sun. For someone who was hot and tired it would be a tempting place to rest.

I tried the handle and the pickup door surprised me by swinging open with scarcely a squeak of its old hinges. Under a layer of Nebraska dust, the seat was intact. It was cracked and it was hard with age, but it was intact. There wasn't even that much dust. Those boys, the rabbit hunters, probably played in the old truck. I know I would have, when I was a boy. Now that I'm an adult, of course, I don't play with trucks.

I dropped my pack so I could slide in and sit behind the wheel. Right. This felt right. I started to grip the wheel—a natural thing to do—but stopped myself. Fingerprints, I thought. There could be fingerprints. I sat there imagining I was Cass Deering, looking through the milky haze of the grimy windshield, hungry, thirsty, but resting. Resting. Looking out. Looking out for what? Sitting here, looking. . . .

When my eyes grew used to the dim light, I caught the gleam of glass on the floorboards. They were Mason jars, three of them. As carefully as I could I picked up each one by its metal rim and read the handwritten label. **Apricots. Pickled Beets. Niagara Grapes.** They had come from the house on the Niobrara, and Cass had eaten from them as she sat here in the old pickup.

Waiting.

Sitting here, waiting. Sick, thirsty, hungry, nodding off to sleep and coming awake again. And waiting for Michael.

They had got this far together. In her mind, Cass was still the novel's heroine and they were still following the plot to the letter, even to staying several days in an empty house. She must have known by then that the story was almost over, and she had been ready. She had known where the next resting place would be, and, if the police didn't catch them there, they might make it to freedom.

Had I been Michael, I would have agreed with her plan. He would have probably assumed the police would find the car, sooner or later, and finding it that far north of Alliance would have led them to think they had been fleeing in that direction. The last thing the police would have expected was that they'd turn around and head south on foot.

Cass had known this part of the county pretty well. If she could have got them past Alliance, they could have hitch-hiked all the way out of the state. But she couldn't have gone much farther without rest. When they had come across the hill, they had found the shed, just as I had done. They had discovered the pickup truck, and she had sunk down on the seat and gone to sleep. Michael probably had watched her sleeping and had seen how sunburned and parched and weak she looked. He evidently had decided to go try to get some water or some more food. Maybe he had decided to go find help, like he had told the truck driver. Or maybe that was an idea that had occurred to him after he had walked a few miles.

So, Michael walked out to the road. But, like me, he had been momentarily disoriented by the fact that it runs east and west, instead of north and south. Let's see, I thought. He probably walked up the road for some distance, thinking he might find a farm. Given his state of mind, after several days of heat and dehydration, he may even have fixed on the idea of walking to Hay Springs. Or back to the farm on the Niobrara where they had found food before.

I climbed out of the deserted truck and picked up my pack and walked out to the road. It was hard to tell which way it ran. But if you wanted to go north, the best bet was to turn right and go that way. I tried it, and, even before I was out of sight of the ruined house, the county road took a sudden ninety-degree turn to the left, and, now, it was clearly headed due north. Michael had gone stumbling along in the heat, his mind probably fixed on finding help for Cass. On he had gone, probably stumbling and falling to his knees in the scorching hot dust and gravel, crying out in frustration, looking back all the time in hope of seeing a car coming through the shimmering heat waves.

I saw a stock tank just off the road and went over to look at it. Michael may have stopped here and plunged his head under the scum-covered water, gulping and gulping his belly full until it hurt. Then he had had to go on, lurching up the road, weaving from the shoulder to the center and back, dragging his feet, feeling the spasms of nausea in his throat. He had come to the drive leading back to the boarded-up house where he and Cass had their last three days of comparative happiness with each other, playing honeymooners. He had been tempted to stop there and rest, but now it was just an empty house. He had had to go on. The tractor lady had seen him going north, and, thinking he was just one of the bums who had broken into her property, she let him go on walking.

Beyond the abandoned house he had come to Highway 87. He had walked until he had come to the bridge over the Niobrara, and, halfway across the span, he dimly had realized it was the same creek they had crossed days ago. He had sat down on the wide railing to rest and was staring down at the water when two trucks had passed each other on the bridge and the blast of wind had sent him toppling down into the willows. Sick, exhausted, all he could tell his rescuer was that he needed to find help.

It fit. This was the wrinkle in Cass's plan. In the novel he would have gone with her. But, instead, he had stumbled back out into the heat, never to return to her. At least that was the way my own imagination was seeing it.

Bob Houghton found me back in the shade of the shed again, hunkered down to study snake and skunk tracks. Generations of them, probably, living in the habitations of man long after the humans had gone.

"Whatta ya got?" he said, and I showed him the canning jars in the pickup truck. If there were fingerprints on them and if they were Cass Deering's, we would know she had been here.

"Lucky thing some kid didn't decide to use them for target practice," he said.

"I almost didn't see them myself," I said. "I wouldn't have, except that I stayed in the truck until my eyes adjusted to the gloom."

When we were back in his Jeep wagon with the air conditioner running, Houghton unfolded a topographical map and pointed out where we were and where the bracelet had been found.

"You know," he said, "I never did believe in that bracelet until now. I thought maybe they had found it somewhere in town, and then had made up that story about rabbit hunting and finding it. No reason for Cass Deering to be walking around 'way out here. I gotta hand it to you, Doc. You've done a helluva job, walking these hills in this heat." He poked his finger at some blue spots on the map. They weren't far from where we were sitting. "Lakes," he said.

"Yeah," I said. "Four, five of them. And they're on a straight line from here to Alliance. She would have had to walk around them."

East of the imaginary line of travel I had created for Cass there were even more sand hill lakes, dozens of them dotting the map in that quadrant. Some of them were labeled with names and some weren't.

"What do you think?" I said.

"If Cass's fingerprints turn out to be on these jars or on this pickup, I'll probably get the county sheriff's department to drag some of the lakes. If she was somewhere between here and Alliance, and she was on dry land, somebody would have found some sign of her by now."

"Wouldn't be much left, by now," I observed.

"No. The boys might get lucky and find a skeleton, some clothing, something like that."

"It's like that story by D. H. Lawrence," I said.

"What's that?" Bob said, wheeling the Jeep onto the county road.

"D. H. Lawrence," I said. "He wrote a story about a girl who walks into a farm pond to kill herself."

"Why would she want to do that?" Bob asked.

"She was feeling abandoned. Her mother had died, and her father had died, and her brothers had sold the farm where she had planned to live the rest of her life. She thought she wanted to be with her mother again and just walked out into the pond to drown. This doctor, though, he saved her."

"Oh," Bob said.

I didn't believe Cass Deering had walked into a pond. Michael had left her. We knew that now. In the novel they would have gone on together. Still, she had come this far. Having eaten what was in the jars and having rested herself, she had decided to go on. If Michael had returned and found her gone, he would have known where she was headed; she had told him. The two of them had been headed there all along.

I now knew their destination. What I *didn't* know was why no one had seen her.

Chapter Twelve

"I like very much to be here," she murmured. "It is so solemn and lonely—after my great happiness— with nothing but the sky above my face. It seems as if there were no folk in the world; and I wish there were not."

Tess of the D'Urbervilles
—Thomas Hardy

I had seen the beer cooler on the back seat when I got into Houghton's Jeep station wagon, but it seemed like bad manners to mention it. Just because I was overheated and dehydrated and sunburned was no reason he should offer me a beer. He turned the Jeep around and headed back to the county road.

"Good job, finding those Mason jars," he said. "The labels match up with the ones you found in the trash barrel, so I'm betting the prints do, when we finish checking them. I think we're goin' to have a trail of clues here."

"So," I said, "Michael died in Chadron."

"Yep. Had a little money on him, but no wallet or I.D. Did I tell you we found what we think is his bag in the trunk of her car? Not much in it other than a change of underwear. It's obvious they spent two or three days in that abandoned house. Probably talking about what they'd say and do if they got caught."

"I didn't see any water at that place," I observed, glancing at the cooler on the back seat. "A human being gets dehydrated quickly out here, with no liquids."

"My idea is that they knew they had to get moving again. Like you said, they didn't have any water."

"Thirst is a terrible thing," I said.

"Don't you think she was getting sick or something?" Houghton said. "Maybe she drank some bad water somewhere and got giardia. Because Michael, you know, *he* was the sick one. But he left her sitting in the pickup under the shed and he took off to look for help or food or water or something. All she had was whatever liquid was in those canning jars."

"And that wouldn't be much. Probably not even twelve ounces, no more than a can of beer holds. A can of beer can help a lot, but a person out in the sun all day needs more than that."

"You know," Houghton went on, oblivious to my subtle suggestions, "he told the truck driver he had to get help. I wonder if that meant Cass was sick."

"But she got up and went on," I pointed out.

"Sometimes it's like that. You get stomach cramps or flu for a couple of days, and then you feel better."

"So where was he from, Michael, I mean?" I had given up trying to wangle a beer out of Houghton.

"That's another strange deal. His father filed a missing persons report in Sterling, Colorado, and the cops down there finally figured out he had hitchhiked to Julesburg and caught the Greyhound."

"The father identified the body?"

"Yeah."

Houghton must have forgotten that he had a beer cooler on the back seat, but I could hear those cold cans clinking and gurgling as we drove.

"The guy is a preacher," he went on. "Some kind of faith

healing church. He waited an awful long time to report his son missing. The kid came back home from South America with some kind of parasites in him and was sickly, but the old man figured God would cure him in his own good time. Then Michael got a letter from Alliance and tossed a couple of things into a bag and took off. Caught the bus and ended up here."

"I see," I said.

"Hey! Here's an interesting wrinkle. When I had the father on the phone, he told me he was the one who married them. Cass and Michael. A home ceremony, before the kid went to South America."

My brain was suffering from dehydration, but things still started to click into place.

"So Cass and Michael were married," I said, "and then he went away to do good works in South America. He gets sick down there, and nobody hears from him for a year or more. Carl Deerfield somehow convinced Cass he was dead or had abandoned her and persuaded her to move in with him. Or he moved in with her. Then Michael comes home sick, and his family doesn't know where Cass is. But he hears from somebody in Alliance. The sister? I'll have to check that out. Did his father say how old that letter was? Whether the family received it before Michael came home, I mean?"

"Nobody asked him," Houghton replied.

"Anyway, suppose somebody who knew the both of them sends a letter, care of Michael's family. He reads it, packs some underwear and a toothbrush, and catches the Greyhound north. He arrives in Alliance and finds out . . . or verifies . . . that Cass is shacked up with her former boyfriend."

"I think it's a fairly logical scenario. A little bit like a soap opera, but it makes some sense to me. Don't forget that Michael is sick as a dog, or so the story goes."

Then add all that dehydration to it, I thought. A beer could have saved him.

"OK," Houghton went on. "So Michael contacts her and tells her where he's been all that time. She does what . . . feels guilty, remorseful, and glad he's back, right?"

"Right."

"So she tells him she'll need a few days to get away from Carl. But when she tells Carl she's leaving, he blows up and gets violent and won't let her go. There's a big fight and she stabs him."

"Then she called Michael, who helped her run away. And somewhere out here, after the car ran out of gas, she starts remembering a book she read and convinces Michael they need to hide in this abandoned house she knows about. When he feels better, they'll try to head south on foot until it seems safe to hitchhike or board a bus or something."

"Whatever," Houghton said.

"But she comes down with giardia or something. Flu, maybe."

"Maybe. It's all speculation at this point. I just want to know whether she got away or whether she's still hiding somewhere on my patch, that's all."

"Surely her sister would have heard from her, if she's hiding with somebody somewhere out here."

"Yeah, but would her sister tell us?"

Houghton slowed down the Jeep to turn onto a weed-covered access road. At the gate he got out and rummaged around the base of a fence post until he came up with a padlock key that opened the chain, then he replaced the key and we drove a few hundred yards into an unplanted field and up a low hill. He set the brake and got out and opened the back door of the Jeep.

"I'm gonna have a beer," he said nonchalantly. "You want one?"

"I guess I could," I said.

He took two cans from the cooler and set them on the Jeep hood. I got out and grabbed mine. He gestured toward a long draw wooded with scrub trees.

"County deputies and volunteers made a sweep," he said, pointing north, "from 'way up there out to the next mile road, then south, clear to the railroad tracks. Nothin'. Those boys, huntin' rabbits, found her charm bracelet right out there."

It was the same kind of terrain I had walked through, marked by low hills, brushy draws, thick windbreaks, and fields of corn and wheat.

"So," I said, "how come they didn't search farther out, say another mile east?"

"The rain had already wiped out any kind of tracks. Besides, we all figured she got away in her car. We only did a foot search because there were two people involved . . . or missing."

"I guess I don't follow you," I said.

"It only takes one person to drive a car. The other one might have been on foot, for all we knew. A missing person search is a funny thing, Doc. Everybody has a different idea what to look for and where to look for it. The best you can hope for is for somebody to find a clue to show you what direction to go."

I drank my beer and surveyed the countryside. I still had the *feeling,* and for some reason the *feeling* seemed to be making me calm and relaxed and a little sad all at the same time. Maybe resigned is the best word for it.

"You know, Bob," I said, "I'm wondering something."

"What's that?" he asked.

"Why Cass went on alone. Why she didn't wait for Michael. I mean we don't know how long she stayed at that shed with the old truck in it, but obviously she finally left there and headed south again. I'm not sure she gave up on him."

"She didn't? So why leave?"

"Maybe . . . this is just speculation . . . maybe she did it to protect him. She might not have known that Carl was really dead, but she had to have realized she was guilty of bodily assault, if not murder. And now Michael was an accessory. Sitting there in that old truck all that time, I'd bet that got her to thinking what kind of trouble he would be in for helping her."

"Could be," Houghton agreed.

"I told you she may have been preoccupied with a novel, particularly with parallels between it and her own situation. Well, in the book the heroine realized she was the one to blame for everyone's trouble. If Cass thought of that . . . the idea probably nagged at her until she couldn't stand it any longer and she ran away."

"OK, Doc, but why avoid the roads? Why did she avoid the search parties and houses, if she felt so responsible? Wouldn't it be more likely that she'd try to get caught or even turn herself in? To save everybody more grief?"

"I don't know. Wait a minute! We're overlooking something pretty obvious here. She could've made it past town and caught a bus or a ride, or she could've found somebody living in some lonely place out here, who would shelter her. But isn't it more likely that she had an accident?"

"Accident?"

"Sure. Look." I pointed out across the hills and valleys where they seemed to stretch beyond the horizon. "You were the one who said she could have fallen into a pond out there. But anything could have happened. She could have been trampled by a range bull, tumbled into an old well, slipped and drowned in an irrigation ditch."

"Sure."

"Or old houses. She's already hidden in that old house up north of here, then the shed with the truck in it. Suppose she got into another deserted ramshackle building somewhere out there, and it fell in on her? I heard of a guy once who was killed because he went into a grain storage bin and the grain avalanched down on him."

"It's possible," Houghton said. "If that's what happened, sooner or later somebody is bound to come across the body. Or the skeleton. I guess I ought to say remains, huh? You want another beer?"

"Only if you're having one," I said.

"I can't," he explained. "We need to get back on the road, and the county has an open container law."

"So if I'm drinking another beer while you drive, you'd have to arrest me?"

"Yep."

Nice guy, I thought.

My theory about why Cass decided to go on alone seemed valid, and my other theories about what might have happened to her also made sense, sort of. But in another respect, it all seemed wrong. The *feeling* was trying to tell me there was something else I needed to remember, some other factor I was overlooking. Something else, some other impulse drew Cass southward, even if she had to go alone. Somehow I knew what it was, but couldn't get it to work its way up out of my unconscious. As we started to get back into the Jeep, I looked across the hills and saw some tall landmarks in the distant haze. I shielded my eyes against the dusty sun glare and tried to make them out.

"What are those?" I asked.

Houghton turned and looked where I was pointing. "Those ones on the right are grain elevators. They're on the railroad, on the south side of town. The other two are the Alliance water towers."

"I remember the water towers, but I would have thought they were farther west. So where's Carhenge, for instance?"

"Let's see," Houghton said. "I guess it's pretty much on a straight line between here and the water tower. Ah! You're thinkin' Cass was a little mixed up, but then she spotted the water towers and headed that way, right?"

"Right," I said, for I did sense it was what she had done. Silently I asked myself why.

I thought I'd get my colleague, Professor Palmer, to help me do some research at the local library, in return for which I would let her buy me a steak, but she had skipped town. According to the note stuck in my trailer door, she had gone to Lincoln to see about her manuscript and she'd phone me on the way back.

No problem. I could always buy my own steak, and the library work wasn't all that complicated. It only took an hour to locate news stories about the murder and the search; I also looked up the weather reports for that week. On the day Cass disappeared, temperatures were above normal and the skies were clear and it stayed that way for the next five days. So I was right. They had been walking through brutal heat. When Michael set out from the shed where the old pickup sat, it was overcast and slightly cooler. The next day saw overcast and scattered showers, and so did the next day. Then things really broke loose when Cass left the shed and continued walking south. There were hard rains and cold winds for most of the next week.

I told Houghton I intended to go back to the place he'd shown me, or even to the shed with the old pickup in it, and continue following Cass's trail on foot. He thought I was as loony as a squirrel on steroids, of course. No use trying to explain to him that I was following a feeling and was hoping I could *see* or *feel* where she had gone. He did agree, however, to telephone the landowners and get permission for me to walk across their property. I guess he thought it might save him the trouble of driving out there to arrest a trespasser.

Houghton didn't have any luck with the men who owned the two farms just north of Carhenge. One of them lived about twenty miles north of Alliance, and Houghton couldn't get hold of him. The other one was an old boy who didn't like anybody stomping around in his crops. I decided to drive out there and see about it in person.

The instant I turned Horse off the highway and into the farm lane, the place reminded me of my grandfather's old homestead back in Colorado. There were the same lilac bushes making a thick hedge along the lane, the same big expanse of dirt called "the yard" where tractors and trucks and pieces of farm equipment were parked, even the same chickens pecking at the gravel under the watchful eye of the same sleepy border collie. A couple of farm cats that were sunning themselves in the middle of the yard leaped up and dashed away when I drove in. On my right I saw a picket fence, more lilacs, a small lawn, and the back porch door of the farmhouse.

As I got out of the pickup, I saw the farmer coming toward me from the barn and I walked that way, meeting him halfway. He seemed like a nice enough old character. Better yet, he was unarmed. He acknowledged Houghton's call about me and invited me to step over into the shade of the building to talk.

It wasn't that he didn't like outsiders, he explained. The problem, he said, was that most people don't know how to walk through crops without wrecking them. He proceeded to tell me, in great detail, about pheasant hunters who shot their guns toward the house, and tourists who walked out into the wheat and stomped it all down while they took pictures, and little old ladies who stole corn to feed their squirrels. Eventually he started to run out of examples. I thought about asking him if he ever had had a professor walk through his fields, following a fictitious heroine. But I didn't ask; I don't want to be known as a smart-ass.

While he was talking, I had glimpsed a car sitting in the shed behind him. It was covered up with a tarp, but I could see that it had a boxy shape and tires that looked like the big old-fashioned type, so I guessed it to be a classic of some kind. Why else protect it with a tarp? Anyway, a long time ago I learned one of the best ways to get on the good side of a man is to ask him about his car. If you're in a bar in a small town and want to strike up a conversation, ask the guy on the stool next to you how his car is running. Either that or ask about his hemorrhoids.

"Looks like you've got an old-timer stored over there," I observed casually.

"Oh, that's my baby!" he said. "Y'oughta see her. C'mon!"

He led me over to the shed and pulled back the tarp to uncover an old Plymouth, a four-door sedan. I didn't know the year, but it was one of those body designs they used to call "a box sitting on a box". It's hard to believe this squat-looking, square car was actually the predecessor of the streamlined Plymouth Barracuda.

"What year?" I asked.

"That's a Nineteen Fifty model," he said proudly. "I got 'er back in Nineteen Sixty and kinda let 'er go to hell over the years, but, lately, I've been restoring her. Takes a lot of time an' work, but, like the wife says, it keeps me offen the streets."

"Hard to find parts, I imagine," I said.

"You got no idea," he said. "Not so much hard to find, but god-awful expensive."

"There's a kid in Alliance . . . ," I said. "Ronnie Webber? He says he knows every car in the whole county, junked or running. I'll bet he'd know where some parts are."

"I know Ronnie. He got me that bumper."

The farmer touched the front bumper with his foot, then turned and pointed to a sanded and varnished length of 2x6 lumber leaning against the wall of the shed.

"That plank, there, was my bumper for ten years, believe it or not. Made it myself. Bent up the original one gettin' pulled out of a ditch. One day in town, that kid, Ronnie, he was lookin' at my home-made wood bumper and said he'd find me a real one. And he did, too. Cost me fifty bucks, but it's worth it."

I hunkered down to admire the wide whitewalls on the car's big tires.

"Haven't seen big wide whitewall tires like these in years," I said. "I used to hate 'em. I worked in a Conoco station where we washed cars, and my job was to scrub the whitewalls. Charged fifty cents extra. That was for all four, of course."

I ran my hand over the broad white band, remembering the summers I spent working in the Conoco station. We washed cars by hand and the boss inspected every job personally. We had to wash everywhere, even up inside the wheel wells and behind the bumpers. I looked at the inside of the Plymouth's front bumper and saw vestiges of battleship gray paint. The color that was used to paint Carhenge.

"Somebody painted your bumper once upon a time," I said.

"Yeah, I saw that," he said. "When the kid brought it, he had it all shined up and purty, but there was this gray primer paint on the inside. It don't show, so I don't mess with it."

After spending twenty minutes admiring how he had fixed up the interior and another half hour hearing how much trouble and expense he had gone to in general, I managed to turn the conversation around to the topic of Cass's crossing his place.

"So the search parties didn't find any sign of her out there on your land, I guess?"

"They didn't look. *I* did. Don't like people stompin' around in my fields. They came by and told me what they was lookin' for, so I told 'em I'd go look and tell 'em if I found anything. Took my tractor and drove all over, the whole place, every corner and fence line and ditch. Never saw a sign of anybody or anything. 'Course, you understand, it rained all that week. Good thing I got a cab on my tractor. Back in the old days, we were lucky if we had one of them umbrellas over the seat. We only used 'em f'r shade. If it rained, we got wet, that's all. Now we got cabs an' air conditionin' and everything."

I was getting the picture. Sitting more than six feet up off the ground, in a glassed-in tractor cab, in rain, he had searched and found no tracks. I wasn't surprised. I noticed he also wore trifocals.

He condescended to climb into Horse with me and show

me where I could drive along his fence line to the end of his property. We bumped along the two-rut track while he told me how much trouble and expense a man had in maintaining his roads and raising crops, and he was still talking when we came to his southeast corner. I got out and put a hand to a fence post and looked south. He went on talking about equipment repairs and the price of fertilizers, but I tuned him out.

The neighboring field, neglected and fallow, sloped gently to a soft rise. Just barely peeking over the rise were the tops of the lintels of Carhenge, the car bodies that had been welded across other cars set upright in the earth. From this distance they looked like capstones on a Neolithic burial site, remnants of a prehistoric defense against the unpredictable forces alive in those awesome empty plains. Over to the left were the cars of the Fourd Seasons sculpture, reaching up out of the horizon like faraway sarsens or obelisks. If I squinted my eyes it was like looking at the Salisbury Plain of England with its "standing stones" rising from the sod.

I felt the *feeling* again. It told me Cass had been here and had seen distant Carhenge. More than that—she was *expecting* to see it. Ever since leaving the rotting pickup in the tumbledown shed, her steps had surely been directed straight toward the place.

"Do you know who owns that land between here and Carhenge?" I asked.

"Sure," he said. "That'd be Harold Mueller. He lives up by Hemingford now. If you wanted to walk on his place, he wouldn't care. Wouldn't even know about it, probably. Go ahead an' take your walk, but you better hope Mueller don't find you there."

"I thought you said he wouldn't care. What does he

do, shoot trespassers?" I asked.

"Nah," my host said, "he's a pussycat. Trouble is he talks all the time. If you was to run into him out there, he'd just plain talk y'to death, Mueller would. Why, one time I remember he came to the house. . . ."

Back in town I went to the Homesteader where I slid into an empty booth rather than taking a stool at the bar. It caused Ed to ask me if I was all right when he brought me my mug of beer.

"Just fine." I smiled.

The truth was there are certain times when I'm in the mood to sit at a bar with the other guys and swap Cornhusker or Bronco forecasts, and there are other times when I want to lean back against the Naugahyde and stare off into space or watch the condensation sliding down the side of the beer mug to make a puddle on the table. I guess you'd call it thinking, for lack of a better term.

Ed must have taken it as a sign of despondency or something, because he came back over to me carrying one of those little bags of potato chips, which he set down next to my beer.

"Here you go," he said. "Have a snack. On the house."

What a big old sentimental lug he was turning out to be.

Ronnie Webber walked in out of the glare of day just as I was starting my second beer. He glared around like he expected somebody to challenge him to a fight right there and then until he was satisfied that he had pretty much intimidated everybody in the place. Everybody included Ed, two guys sitting at the end of the bar, and me. He moved toward a stool.

"Ron!" I called. "Over here."

He signaled that he had seen me, got a draw from Ed,

and joined me in the booth.

"What's up?" I asked.

"Nuthin' much. I got an eighteen-wheeler back up on the road this morning. The driver didn't think my wrecker would handle it, but I showed him. Nuthin' else happenin'. Price of gas went down another cent."

"I wanted to ask you a favor," I said. "Maybe tomorrow night you could drive me out to Zimmer's place, or just this side of it, and drop me off. I could pay you for your time."

"You wanna be dropped off on foot, that far from town?" He looked incredulous.

"Yep. Suppose you could help me out?"

"Sure. What time?"

"Whenever. After supper. Maybe you'd come by the trailer when you're ready."

"You got it."

"I've been meaning to ask you. . . ." I signaled for Ed to bring us two more beers.

"Yeah?"

"Ol' man Zimmer showed me his 'Fifty Plymouth."

"Yeah?"

Ed set down the frosty mugs and I waited until he was out of earshot behind the bar again.

"Zimmer told me about the bumper you got him. Just between you and me, and I sure don't give a damn, that bumper came from Carhenge, right?"

"What if it did?"

"Don't matter to me, like I said. But you already know I've been prowling around out there. Well, north of there anyway. I'm pretty interested in the way Cass Deering disappeared. The thing is," I went on, trying to make it sound confidential, "I think I can pick up her trail at Zimmer's place and follow it across Mueller's place. I'll probably end up at Carhenge, see? And just between you and me, that place scares the hell out of me. People tell me stories about ghosts and packs of wild dogs . . . all kinds of stuff. What's-her-name, the lady at the Laundromat, even believes there have been aliens out there. So when Zimmer told me about the bumper, I figured you'd been there at night. You know what I mean. Did *you* ever run across anything scary or strange out there?"

I thought I was putting on a pretty good act, playing up to Ronnie's overblown sense of his own importance, and I was right. His response to my rôle as a timorous out-of-towner was better than I could have hoped.

"Tell you what," he said, leaning forward over the table to speak in hushed tones. "That night I got that bumper, that was the last time I'm goin' near that death car. 'Specially at night."

"Death car?" I asked.

"That 'Fifty Plymouth welded up there on top, across those two Ford wagons."

"That's the death car?"

"Sure, that's it. That night I got the bumper off of it, the wind was blowing like hell. Big ol' blasts of it came from all over the place, blowin' this way, that way, hard enough t'rip your head off. I climbed up on that Colony Park wagon to get to the Plymouth . . ."—and Ronnie halted abruptly. "Hey, you gonna tell Houghton about this?"

"No way," I said. "You've got my word on it. But how come you were out there in that kind of weather, anyway?"

"Just bein' dumb, I guess. I figured if it was rainin' and dark, then the cops wouldn't bother to drive out there. I just didn't figure on all that wind."

"So what happened? You said you wouldn't do it again."

"OK. Just don't you say nuthin' to anybody. So, I

climbed up the frame on that Ford, like I said, carryin' a little flashlight in my teeth, until I could work my way around back of the Plymouth and stand on the other Ford's tailgate. Had one foot on the tail light and one on the bumper. All I had with me was two wrenches and a bunch of sockets in my pocket, and the flashlight. Oh, and a cheater bar. That's all I had. So, I'm up there in all this wind, see, tryin' to blow me the hell off that station wagon, feelin' up behind the bumper to get a socket on the nuts, and all over the place there's loose sheet metal bangin' and crashin' back and forth. Man, you never heard such a racket. And that ol' Ford I'm standin' on, she's rockin' in the wind, see? So, I put the cheater bar on the wrench and got three nuts off. There's only one more, but it's stuck really good. So I hunch my shoulders up into the wheel well to brace myself, and I start hammerin' away on the end of that cheater bar with my other wrench. Bam! Bam! Bam! And that wind blowing sand and shit, and metal bangin' around. Then I heard it, see."

"Heard it," I repeated. "Heard what?"

"That moanin' noise. Y'know those videos where a ghost or somethin' comes up some old hallway and he's got his arms up and goin' whoo, whooooo?"

Ed and the two guys at the bar looked around at us when Ronnie demonstrated the ghost.

Ronnie put his arms down and leaned forward again. "Well, anyway, you know. That whooo noise."

"It came from the death car?" I asked.

"Hell, I didn't know. And I didn't care, neither! All I wanted was t'get that nut off, grab that bumper, and get outta there. Man, I was shakin' all over by the time I got down off those cars. I don't care what anybody's offerin' for Plymouth parts, I ain't goin' back near that one for nuthin'."

"So when was this, do you think? What I mean is was this about the same time as the murder?"

"I dunno. Might have been. No. Hell, I dunno. I know I was out there one other night, right around the same time I got the bumper, and I had to dodge Houghton's prowl car. One of the cops, anyway. Seemed to be goin' by Carhenge every hour or so."

Well, three beers and one ghost story made a pretty good end to my afternoon. I paid the tab, then walked through the early evening quiet of the town's streets toward the trailer park. A few cars drove by, taking their owners home to supper after a day's work. I noticed, with a smile, that people were beginning to recognize me as a sort of fixture— the professor crazy enough actually to walk more than two blocks in the midsummer Nebraska heat. Women driving past me would dip their heads in a little bow as a friendly greeting; the men generally lifted an index finger off the top of the steering wheel, the standard automotive salute out in that country. Back home in the city you either get the other finger or drivers pretend they don't see you at the same time they're trying to run you down. When you encounter these same fossil-fueled assassins at a faculty reception or when they're trying to sell you time shares or insurance plans, they're all grins and hearty handshakes.

All things considered, I much prefer the little nods and the friendly salute with the index finger. I like the way small town drivers yield the right-of-way at intersections and drive slowly on the streets, in case someone is backing out of their driveway. That's why I wondered what I did, as I walked under the old elms where birds twittered softly and overstuffed cats watched me from wooden porch steps. Was I really trying to clear up a mystery because I felt I *had* to? Or, was I just using Cass's disappearance as an excuse to stay here a while longer?

I was sure of one thing: wherever Cass had gotten to, it was a pretty safe bet that she was wishing she was back here on these shady streets again.

Chapter Thirteen

Into my heart an air that kills
From yon far country blows:
What are those blue remembered hills,
What spires, what farms are those?

That is the land of lost content,
I see it shining plain,
The happy highways where I went
And cannot come again.
"A Shropshire Lad"
—A. E. Housman

"Are you sure you really want to do this, Doc?"

Ronnie turned off the engine and we both got out. We were at the end of the dirt road between Zimmer's land and the Mueller place. The sun was down but the sky was still light enough that we could see the big bank of heavy clouds off to the southwest. Blue zigzags of lightning cut through the dark gray mass from time to time.

"This storm probably won't amount to much," I said. Probably the same thing the *Titanic*'s captain had said about the iceberg.

Ronnie knit his eyebrows together in an effort to look knowledgeable about weather patterns. "Looks like it'll go on north, a long ways west of town. Might get a few little drops, that's all," he said confidently.

I had a good poncho in my pack and good hiking boots,

so I wasn't worried. Cass Deering probably made the same walk in similar weather, wearing street shoes or sandals, and possibly a light jacket or sweater. Even if I ran into bad weather on my little hike, I thought, it could turn out to be advantageous. In good weather, if she proved my theory by sticking to the plot of the novel, Cass made straight for Carhenge to hide and decide what to do. But if she had got caught in the rain somewhere along the way, maybe she had looked around and seen a barn or shed or something, maybe even a wooded gully or culvert. If the overcast turned into a downpour, I'd probably do the same thing.

All of this reminded me of the time I had trudged around in the woods and heath on the Isle of Mull in Scotland following the *feeling* in hopes of it leading me to a lost manuscript. Here I was again, traipsing around outdoors following a hypothesis and a hunch.

"You sure you don't want me t'pick you up at th' other end?" Ronnie asked, interrupting my thoughts.

"No," I said. "I'm OK. Once I get to Carhenge, I'll just walk or hitchhike into town. You go ahead. Take off."

He got back into his pickup, made a U-turn in the field, and headed back down the road. The sound of the engine became faint and fainter and faded away, leaving me once again alone with the rolling sweep of hills, the lowering leaden sky, and the question. The grayness and the silence pulled at me; I wanted to get going immediately because the walking would make me feel better, more secure. Just to stand here, unmoving, was scary, to tell the truth, but to hurry off across the fields wouldn't be the thing to do. Getting started on this walk would certainly distract my mind from the immensity of space and sky, but first I needed to clear my mind and focus on what I was supposed to be doing. I sat down at the edge of the untended field and waited. And watched. And listened.

Instead of thinking about the loneliness of the place, I focused on my breathing and consciously relaxed my muscles. I waited until my mind became calm enough to focus on the small details of my surroundings. Tiny sounds came to me from out of the grass, sounds of insects and movement. The clean scent of bare earth rose to mingle with aromas of wild grass and dry wheat straw. A light breeze, sharp-edged and lightly moist, came from the direction of the storm, and, if I walked directly into it, I would pass under the clouds and into town. If I were to keep the breeze touching my left cheek and steer by the beacon far away on top of a water tower, I would get back to the highway near Carhenge.

I stood up, careful not to abandon the sense of relaxation. I let it flow down my belly and into my legs, imagining watching myself standing there, watching myself breathe evenly and ease myself into the evening, ease my thoughts into the patterns and texture of the place.

There! I saw it! If I had been standing ten steps away in either direction, I would have missed it. If I had just taken off walking down the field, I would have missed it. But there it was, a silhouette of a far-off structure growing more distinct the more I looked at it. It was Carhenge, distant and barely visible at a certain spot between two hills. It looked like a miniature village glimpsed through a fold of earth.

I turned to look back toward Zimmer's place and imagined Cass crossing all that country to the north. Mentally I replayed her walk like a film running backward, seeing her stumbling through the hollow between hills where her charm bracelet was found, seeing her at the collapsed house with the pickup abandoned in the shed. I saw her sleeping in the big house all boarded up and empty, envisioned her sneaking past the farm on the Niobrara River, crossing the fence at the junkyard where they had left her car.

At that moment, standing in the Nebraska twilight, every sense I had was telling me I was standing in Cass Deering's footprints, that she had passed this way. My own line of march was obvious: I would walk down the gentle hill, then down between the two low hills farther on, and into Carhenge. I could already sense Cass's fatigue and isolation and the single focus of her mind as she had stood where I was standing. From here she had pointed her steps toward distant Carhenge, but what did she think she would do then? If she had seen the place from here, had it given her hope or a sense of finality? The novel would end at Carhenge, leaving her without a story.

Surely she had known that. So what else had been leading her there? Something in my mind, some memory somewhere inside all the synapses and processes was trying to swim into focus. Something was trying to make itself known to me, trying to rise up out of the pool of dim memories and materialize in my consciousness.

I started walking. With that wall of storm clouds rising higher against the sky, the darkness was rapidly thickening.

The first big drops smacked into me before I had gone a quarter mile. I took out the poncho and put it on, the gusting wind already strong enough to whip the fabric around and make it hard to snap the edges together. By the time I had the snaps closed, the drawstring at my waist tightened and the hood up, heavy drops were pattering all over me like rain on a tent. The hood pulled tightly around my face was already cold and clammy; it kept me from looking to left or right, too, cutting off my peripheral vision so that I truly was focused on the distant circle of car bodies. I could not see it, most of the time, with the rain coming and the darkening skies; I could only imagine where it was, out there in the far distance.

The fallow fields I was attempting to cross must have been planted with corn or sugar beets at one time, for there were overgrown hills separated by regularly spaced furrows. The hills were thick with tough weeds and plant stubs, and the furrows were slippery with mud. Each time I tried to make a stride, my foot came down either on a twisted clump of roots or skidded on the side of a muddy furrow, throwing me off balance. I tried taking big steps from ridge to ridge, sticking to the higher and firmer places, but the hills of dirt would break off and threaten to drop me on my butt. The way I was lurching from side to side, waving my arms under the poncho for balance, not to mention the wind whipping the poncho around, I must have looked like a demented scarecrow flapping along in a green sheet.

With my luck, somebody would spot me and call Bob Houghton to report a spook, and he'd come out and empty a shotgun at me.

The rain now angled down in sheets and I bent my head into it, seeing only a few feet of ground directly ahead of my boots. I no longer knew whether I was walking in a straight line or making a huge circle. All I knew for certain was that I was walking downhill, more or less. The field sloped even more and I went on and on until I thought I *was* going in circles. Water standing in the furrows made the field more like a shallow lake with weeds sticking up out of it. Raindrops smacked into the standing water like miniature cannonballs, splashing in all directions. Muddy rainwater came to the tops of my boots and poured in, and from the knees down my soaked jeans weighed like lead.

"At least there's no lightning," I muttered, bending to

force myself forward against the rain coming down like razors of cold water.

That, of course, was when a gigantic bolt of electricity lit up the sky like noonday. At nearly the same instant I heard the boom of thunder and vibrations running through the ground. My heart seemed to stop, then it started racing; I found myself in a crouch without remembering that I had crouched, as if by making myself a foot or two shorter I would be safe.

The flash of lightning had one good effect, at least. It showed the edge of that damned field. In a few moments, I was out of the old furrows and was standing in wild, deep grass, soaking wet grass that waved and slashed back and forth in the shifting winds.

Another bolt of lightning lit up the area. There was a barbed-wire fence ahead of me, about fifty yards, and then it was a clear slope down to Carhenge. Why the hell did I take comfort in knowing I was close to a circle of steel cars in a lightning storm?

More thunder boomed and growled, the echo going on and on as if it would never cease reverberating across the prairie hills. I had started this walk by relaxing my mind and controlling my breathing; now I caught myself holding my breath altogether.

I stumbled and slid my way through the mud and grass to reach the fence. Working for the U.S. Forest Service years ago, I had learned the hard way that lightning loves barbed wire. I had been stretching the last section of a drift fence and putting in the last few staples when a jolt of lightning over a ridge hit the other end of the fence and the electricity came a half mile along the wire. Even though I had been wearing heavy leather gloves at the time, I felt the numbness in my arm for two days afterward.

When I got to the fence, I looked for a gate or opening. I considered making some kind of heroic, graceful vault over it by running, placing one hand atop a fence post, and lightly swinging myself over. Yeah. Sure. Wearing a flopping wet poncho, boots saturated with ten pounds of water, not to mention the weight of my blue jeans at this point, I was going to vault a five-strand fence. I could have climbed up over a post, using the strands of wire as steps, but that would have given the lightning my butt for a target.

I wrestled around inside the poncho until I got the pack off, which I tossed over the fence. And then, figuring that I was already so wet and muddy it didn't matter, I lay down on my belly and slithered under the bottom wire. I wonder, I thought, if doing this is really, really better than being at one of Aggie's sherry parties or attending the opening of the concert season?

It's funny, the thoughts that come into your head sometimes. Squirming under the fence in the mud like a G.I. in one of those WWII movies, I suddenly remembered I had forgotten to call Aggie before leaving my trailer. I wondered if she was worried about me. I knew *I* was.

I stood up, soaked and caked with mud, and a hard blast of chilling wind nearly blew me flat again. I twisted away from it, putting up my arm to shield my face from the needles of wind-driven rain. I felt the cold in my arm, and on my face, and the shiver crawling up my back told me that hypothermia was a very real possibility here. The thunder boomed again and the lightning lit up the field around me. Again I could feel the vibrations through my boots.

More wind pushed those needles of cold rain straight into me. Again it twisted me, and again I put my arm across my face, only this time my foot skidded on a muddy hummock and I fell right on top of what must have been the

only remaining piece of obdurate rock in the sand hills. My hip felt on fire. I pictured a bruise the size of a dinner plate spreading from waist to thigh.

I got up and crouched into the wind, the poncho flailing at me. Off to my right, not far away, the lightning revealed three car bodies stuck in the hilltop, with two more cars welded end to end so they stuck up twenty or thirty feet. What did the sculptor call it? The Fourd Seasons, after Vivaldi? Very funny. It made a perfect lightning rod. Near the Fourd Seasons on top of the hill was an upright car frame from which hung three huge iron wind chimes clanging maniacally in the gale.

I stumbled away from it, moving blindly forward in the dark rain, straining to see ahead of me, and half expecting to walk over the edge of an abyss. But there was no abyss. Instead, there came a sudden drop in the wind, and at the same instant I came up against one of the cars hulking up black and solid in the darkness. The next flash of lightning illuminated the car for a split second, showing the sheet metal welded over the windows and the hood pointing upward into the clouds. Rain still hammered down, but at least the car blocked the wind.

Lightning and steel, I thought as I caught my breath. Electricity and water everywhere. Well, I was into it now. I tried the fatalistic approach by telling myself I wouldn't hear the one that killed me, but instantly wondered if that were true. When John Wayne says—"Relax, kid, you won't hear the one that gets you."—he's usually referring to artillery shells, not lightning. With lightning, I thought, you probably hear it, feel it, and survive it long enough to regret it.

The next long flash showed two more cars off to my left and another car on top of them, set across their bumpers like a lintel over a doorway. The wind hammered at them.

From every quadrant of the circle came the racket of sheet metal flapping and banging. I listened in fascinated horror; it was as though I had stumbled into some kind of dark demonic foundry where imps and devils labored in perpetual night, hammering out suits of armor for the legions of hell. The only reassuring thing about it was that the lightning storm seemed to be moving north, away from Carhenge.

Funny, the things that occur to you at the darnedest times. Like forgetting to call home. As I leaned against the shelter of the car, expecting to become the world's largest charcoal briquette at any moment, I realized I should have left Horse here in the parking lot of Carhenge. With a little foresight, he would be only 100 yards away, with a dry cab and a good heater. With a little more foresight there could be a thermos of hot coffee on the seat.

I missed my truck. The Carhenge circle was a clattering chaos of hostile forms among which I was small, exhausted, and all alone. Right now I missed the protection of Horse more than ever before. I felt guilty, too, for leaving the old Dodge out of the adventure, for not giving him a chance to be there for me. There I was, Professor David L. McIntyre B.A. M.A. Ph.D., standing in ankle-deep water, poncho flapping in the storm, wet to the skin, thoroughly chilled, feeling guilt over an inanimate assortment of metal and rubber. But let's face it, there are times when nothing seems better than to be safe and cozy in your own vehicle.

That's when that nagging half memory came bobbing up to the surface of my mind—that thing someone had said. The *feeling* gave a leap of recognition that the storm fittingly accompanied with an explosion of lightning and thunder that illuminated all of Carhenge. Suddenly I knew what else had brought Cass Deering here. I knew what I'd been trying to remember. And I had a good idea where to find her.

★ ★ ★ ★ ★

The wind picked up from a new direction, but the rain was lessening and the lightning was going farther north as the storm moved away. In the light of one flash I saw my next objective: straight across the circle of upright cars were the two tall Ford station wagons with the old Plymouth welded across on top of them—the Country Squire and the Colony Park and the death car. I hurried across the circle, halfway thinking the lightning might spot me if I dawdled out in the open, and squeezed myself in between the upright station wagons. With the Plymouth overhead it was the driest place anywhere around.

It was nothing like being in Horse's cab, but at least the rain couldn't get at me. The wind diminished rapidly, the bodies of the two station wagons blunting the force of what little remained. The Plymouth overhead kept the rain off, so I pulled down the hood of my poncho. Then I took off the pack again and rummaged inside it for my water bottle and my flashlight. Good for Aggie—when it's my birthday and she can't remember the name of my favorite single malt Scotch, she buys me a flashlight, instead. And she doesn't go cheap, either. This year she had bought me a solid aluminum, waterproof, five-cell, krypton-bulb beauty.

I shone it around my hiding place, narrow as a broom closet. The doors of the station wagons were welded shut with sheet metal riveted over the windows, presenting a smooth surface all the way up to the bumpers. Then the beam of the flashlight caught the nameplate on the side of one of the station wagons. It was a scroll of metal letters. Once chrome, probably, it was painted gray like everything else at Carhenge. In the krypton beam it was easy to read: **Country Squire** it said. It was the same year and model as the station wagon in the photograph.

I reasoned that Cass Deering knew Carhenge. She probably had often seen the Country Squire—just like her father's—there with its nose buried in the earth. When she was sitting alone in that abandoned pickup, sick and a little out of her mind, she must have thought about the car of her childhood, the warm and sheltering back seat of her father's Country Squire. She had been through a tragedy that had left her mind numb; she had endured long days of hiding and walking, long nights of shivering with nightmares. In part of her mind she was still the heroine of Hardy's novel, walking toward Stonehenge. But in another part of her mind, she knew where there was a car just like the one she had known as a girl, her favorite childhood refuge. The thought of it had kept her going despite the chills and hunger, and finally had brought her to this point.

I lifted the water bottle to drink, and as I tilted my head back I recalled that poem, "Mr. Flood's Party", by Robinson. One of the loneliest poems in the English language. In the dark, Mr. Flood trudges up a hill from a forsaken hut "that held as much as he should ever know on earth again of home." He stops and talks to himself and offers himself a drink from a jug he's carrying, and then another.

There was not much that was ahead of him,
And there was nothing in the town below—
Where strangers would have shut the many doors
That many friends had opened long ago.

Like Eben Flood I raised my water bottle in a toast. I was going to toast the Country Squire station wagon and say: "Well, Squire, here we are." But in a more somber and serious mood, I lifted the bottle to the darkness and toasted the distant aura of Alliance's lights just over the horizon.

"Well, Cass Deering," I said softly, "here we are."

The storm continued to diminish. So did the thrashing and banging of sheet metal and the moaning of the wind haunting that gray circle of bizarre shapes. The night became so quiet I could hear water dripping from the Plymouth overhead. The last cloud of the storm drifted away from a three-quarter moon that now cast eerie shadows everywhere. The city's luminosity reflected off the departing cloud, occasionally slashed with long streaks of far-off sheet lightning.

I stepped around the Country Squire to look out across the monument at the uprights and lintels on the other side. For just an instant, standing there in my poncho, I might have been a druid at Stonehenge. For just an instant, the cars became the monoliths, the bluestones and sarsens; for an instant they could have been the altar stones and trilithons gathered into a mysterious silent monument on Salisbury's wide and empty Plain. Instead of a flashlight, I could have been holding a pine-knot torch in one hand and a dagger in the other, the bronze blade thirsting for the sacrifice to stain it.

Thunder whoomed far to the north, like a warning more than a departure.

"OK," I said to myself, shaking off the eerie sense of standing within the sarsen circle of Stonehenge. "Let's do this and get the hell out of here."

I stripped off the poncho and dropped it alongside the pack, then used the flashlight to see if I could figure out a climbing route up the chassis of the Country Squire. There was a body mount that would make a good foothold, then I could step on that cross member and get a grip on the next body mount, then the shock absorber bracket, and then the axle.

It worked out just about that way. I climbed up a few feet, using the light to find more handholds, climbed a few more feet, and, finally, by trusting the rusted gas tank with my weight, I was able to haul myself up onto the tailgate. There was more room up there than it appeared from the ground; the Plymouth was not actually resting on the pair of station wagons, but was supported on four upright legs of angle iron.

I turned the flashlight beam toward the rear of the Plymouth to look at the brackets that once held the bumper. Someone had removed it, all right, but there was no telling how long ago. It was easy to see how he would have been able to climb up here and then move over to the other station wagon. From there all he had to do was slide out along the rear door to reach the bumper.

I squirmed around and got more or less comfortable on top of the Country Squire's tailgate, ten or twelve feet off the ground. At least it was dry up here. In fact, it was a pretty good shelter.

Because of the angle iron support reaching down into the interior of the wagon, there was no rear window, just a big dark opening. I shone the light down inside and saw the rear-facing seat. I thought about two little girls playing with dolls there, when the station wagon still had the new car smell and was all shiny and big and powerful. Back where the adults couldn't see them, they could have giggled and sung songs and made up stories about their dolls; they could have curled up into little balls and slept, putting perfect child-like faith in the father driving the big car to get them home safely. Or they could have gone into the garage on warm days, when he had left the back window rolled down, and climbed into their secret back compartment of the station wagon. Just to be there. It was *the* safe place, the hiding place, the place to go when you didn't want to be anywhere else.

I suppose I expected to find Cass there on that little backward facing seat, curled up in death. That would have been the easy way to have it. But despite the fact that the *feeling* was everywhere around me now, she wasn't there.

I stuck the flashlight under my belt and leaned into the window opening, stretching down far enough to reach the back of the seat. It was loose. Each side of it had a latch so the seat back could be folded down to make a flat cargo compartment, but one of those latches had come away from the rusted wheel well. I pulled the back of the seat toward me and the other latch broke off easily. I hung there, lying with my hips and stomach on the tailgate and both arms stretched down to hold the seat back, peering down into thick dank darkness. For a moment I was tempted to leave it that way, just to tell myself that my theory about Cass's having climbed into the back seat of this station wagon had been wrong and let it go at that. Even as I let go of the seat with one hand and reached for my flashlight, I knew I didn't want to find anything else.

The light showed that something had broken the supports holding the backrest of the middle seat. It hung downward like an open trap door in a theatre stage. The front seat was missing altogether, with just the mounting brackets to show where it had been. The steering wheel was also missing, but the steering column was still in place, a thick post with the shift lever broken off. I moved the light a few inches. No engine. The firewall was gone and the engine was gone, so the cavity underneath the dashboard of the Country Squire went all the way to the front grill, four or five feet under the ground.

The engine compartment was a mess of rain water,

chunks of dirty brown stuffing from the seats, shreds of headliner and carpeting, and snarls of wiring and tubing. Among the sodden débris I saw what I knew I would see. Remains of some fabric snagged on jagged metal, a skull and a skeletal hand.

The remains of Cass Deering.

Chapter Fourteen

"Justice" was done, and the President of the Immortals, in Aeschylean phrase, had ended his sport with Tess. . . . The two speechless gazers bent themselves down to the earth . . . and remained thus a long time. . . . As soon as they had strength they arose, joined hands again, and went on.

Tess of the D'Urbervilles
— Thomas Hardy

"McIntyre residence, this is Agatha."

"Hi, Aggie. It's me."

"Oh, David! Where are you? I thought you'd call yesterday! How are you, are you all right? It has been *so* hectic here . . . oh, and I can't talk but a minute. Barbara is coming to pick me up. In fact, I'm standing in the doorway watching for her. Well, how are you? What have you been up to?"

"Mostly hanging around to watch the police wrap up this missing person case," I said. "But it's done now. I would have called yesterday, but I was with the coroner and the sheriff's deputies all day, and then I went out to get a steak with Sergeant Houghton, and, by the time I got back to the trailer, it was pretty late."

"So you're OK?"

"Oh, yeah. Got a big bruise on one hip and scratches from some barbed wire, but I'm OK. Hey, I used my new flashlight, the one you gave me for my birthday. It worked great."

"Oh, I am so glad. I know you like to have a good flashlight with you. That's why I bought it."

"You picked a good one. Listen, I'm going to get Horse's oil changed today, pay my bill at the trailer park, and be ready to head out of here at dawn tomorrow. So I'll be home sometime tomorrow afternoon, if all goes well. OK?"

"Fine! I'll plan something special for dinner. Oh, Barbara just pulled into the driveway! Gotta go! See you tomorrow, then. Love you."

"Love you, too. 'Bye."

That old Nebraska sun had climbed above the trees to hit the front of the trailer, so I moved my folding chair over into the shade next to Horse. He had a stiff-mouth expression on his grill and his headlights looked at me like a kid who's been told he has to quit playing and go home.

"Don't look at me in that tone of voice," I told him. "I said you could have an oil change first. But we're going home, and that's that."

Plenty to do today. I wanted to stop back at the college office and tell Jane Dorner how it had all worked out. She'd read about it in the newspaper, but I felt a little guilty that I hadn't been over there since the summer term ended. Then I had to get Horse's oil changed, stock the cooler with some munchables and fruit for the drive home, check the brakes and the turn signals on the trailer, pay my bill, and say good bye to a few people. Maybe I'd start with a late breakfast down at Houghton's Hut Café.

Maybe I'd run into Ronnie Webber there. Funny kid, Ronnie. Yesterday he came by the trailer to give me $25.

"I forgot," he said, "but here's your change from the money you gave me. When I checked those truck stops, y'know."

It was a pretty obvious bribe. I think Ronnie was afraid I'd say something about the missing bumper now that everybody wanted to talk to me about discovering Cass at Carhenge.

"Keep it," I said. "You drove a lot of miles. Besides, you drove me out to the Mueller place. I think we're even."

"Nah, Doc, I want you to have this money. It's only fair."

"Ronnie, it's OK. Just keep it. I'm leaving in the morning."

Before heading down to the Hut, I needed to make one more call. I tilted my chair back against Horse's fender and punched the number into my cell phone. It was peaceful there in the shade. The morning heat had stifled the sounds of birds and insects and even people. The town seemed as quiet and lonely as at midnight.

"Hello?"

"Hey, Palmer."

"Lachlan. Nice to hear from you. Where are you?"

"Still in Alliance. I'm leaving in the morning. You?"

"Back in Boulder, of course. You did call my home phone number, you know."

"I did? Oh, yeah, I guess I did! So how did it go with Nebraska Press? Are you going to do them a book?"

"*Do* them a book? Great grammar for an English professor! No, I don't think so. We went through the whole dance, though. You know, lunch with one editor and cocktails with another, then dinner with both the next day. And somehow all that talk about my project seemed to make me lose interest in it. As much as I loved it while I was doing it, it's gone stale. I'm into other things now. So I told them thanks for the drinks and conversation, but I'd pass up the opportunity. There's always another book to do, somewhere down the line."

"You're probably right."

"So, did your hunch turn out right?"

"Speaking of crummy grammar. . . ."

"Shut up. I found a copy of *Tess of the D'Urbervilles* and read it while I was in Lincoln. Cass Deering was at Carhenge, wasn't she? Just like Tess ended up at Stonehenge."

"Yeah," I sighed. "She was there. She had climbed up one of those station wagons and had fallen down inside it, all the way to the front grill. The local doctor said she probably died of exposure in there. The coroner agreed with him . . . but I found out that, in Nebraska, they appoint their county attorneys to act as county coroners. They don't necessarily know anything about forensics or pathology."

"She couldn't get out of the car?"

"Evidently not. The doctor found trauma to the skull and a broken arm, and, when we looked at the car again, we all agreed that she probably had hit the steering column when she fell in. Plus, she would have been weak from hunger and hypothermia."

"It's hard to imagine anyone getting hypothermia in the summer."

"The doctor says you can. He says mild hypothermia can set in when your body temperature gets down to ninety-five degrees, especially if the ambient temperature is in the sixties. That's where you start to shiver, get lethargic, start to lose co-ordination, and get confused. Down inside that car, in the rain, lying in a foot or more of water. It must have felt like being inside a food locker. I think she was even confused and possibly in a kind of daze when she climbed up there. I theorized that she was fixated on Tess D'Urberville's flight across the open country and into Stonehenge. Then, when she got close enough to see

Carhenge, she remembered one certain car and wanted to hide there."

"What an awful way to die. Of course, it was awful the way Michael died, too, trying to go for help when he should have been in a hospital."

"It was a Country Squire wagon, like her Dad's. Remember that picture of her and her sister and her dad in front of their new station wagon? Like I told Bob Houghton, I'm sure she had spent time at Carhenge. She must have noticed that Country Squire. It got into her unconscious memory. I remember once, when I was little, I got lost in a big department store. I was with my grandmother, but we got separated somehow. She had introduced me to escalators . . . I had never been on one before . . . and so I went and stood beside the escalator and that's where she found me. Ever since then, when I'm with Aggie or somebody and lose track of them in a store, I automatically look around for an escalator."

"Well, we all know you're weird, Lachlan. She only wanted the comfort of a familiar thing from her childhood, is that it?"

"That's it. I think she tried to climb in the back window so she could curl up on the back seat. If she was still thinking about Hardy's novel, she may have even expected to be found there. The police find Tess at Stonehenge, remember? But one of the seat supports was broken and she rolled off the back of the seat and fell right down through the car. For a few hours she may have moaned and whimpered, maybe even shouted for help, but the weather was so bad nobody was around to hear her. That kid had been there to steal car parts, but that was before all this happened. It's ironic, though . . . while she was suffering a hundred yards from the highway, search parties were looking for her several miles north."

"Poor woman. What a terrible thing to go through.
Well . . . let's talk about something more cheerful, shall we?
I've had a rather hard week, if you're at all interested. Came
home to find the cat missing, the water heater leaking, and
on trash day some dog scattered the contents of two plastic
bags all over my lawn. Oh, and the dean's office has decided to call an emergency meeting of faculty. That includes *you*, too. It's about some kind of budget crisis. I'm
seriously considering deleting his e-mail message and
leaving town that day. Maybe I'll tell them I had to go to a
special historical conference, but I'll just take some wine
and a picnic to the mountains, instead."

"Hey, Palmer! You're starting to sound like *me!*" I
said.

"Lachlan, don't say that. Me, sounding like you! My
God, what a scary thought! I told you I've already had a
tense week. Don't make it worse."

"OK, so I'm sorry. I've had a tough week myself."

"So. I'll see you back in Boulder?"

"Sure. In a couple of days, maybe. We'll do coffee or
something."

"We'll just do the coffee. Something takes in too many
possibilities."

"Fair enough." I laughed. " 'Bye for now."

" 'Bye," she said.

I got up and folded the chair, then put it and the phone
into the trailer. When I came back out, Horse was still
looking grim-grilled and gargoyle-eyed.

"I told you not to look at me in that tone of voice," I
said. "C'mon. Breakfast for me, an oil change for you, and
then we're going to see about getting out of here. If you give
me any trouble, I'll just leave you at Carhenge and you can

spend the rest of your days buried nose downward in north-east Nebraska."

The V-8 purred politely as the shift lever slid, smooth as silk, into second gear. Breakfast and a lube job would postpone the departure a little longer, but both Horse and I knew it was time.

Time to move on. Time to pack up the books and notes, hitch up the trailer, and just move on.

And nothing now remained to do
But begin the game anew.
"A Shropshire Lad"
—A. E. Housman

About the Author

James C. Work was born in Colorado where his family has lived for four generations. His mother's grandparents were in Leadville and Cripple Creek during the gold rush days, while his father's forebears were pioneer farmers on Colorado's eastern plains. He grew up in Estes Park and attended Colorado State University and the University of New Mexico, and holds degrees from both. He taught literature at Colorado State University.

Western American literature first heard of Work in 1984 when he took on the job of restoring Jack Schaefer's novel *Shane* for the University of Nebraska Press. Since then he has published *Prose and Poetry of the American West*, an anthology which won the Colorado Seminars in Literature Annual Book Award. Of the 100 or so essays he has written, a sampling can be found in *Following Where the River Begins*. This work won the Charles Redd Award in Western Studies. He was also the editor of a collection of short stories titled *Gunfight!* which includes many stories by Western favorites. *Ride South to Purgatory* (Five Star Westerns, 1999), the first book in his Keystone Ranch saga, was his first Western novel. The saga also includes *Ride West to Dawn* (Five Star Westerns, 2001), *Ride to Banshee Cañon* (Five Star Westerns, 2002), and *The Dead Ride Alone* (Five Star Westerns, 2004). His next **Five Star Western** will be *Deathwater Valley*.